Walt Disney's Donald Duck

• To Well and Back •

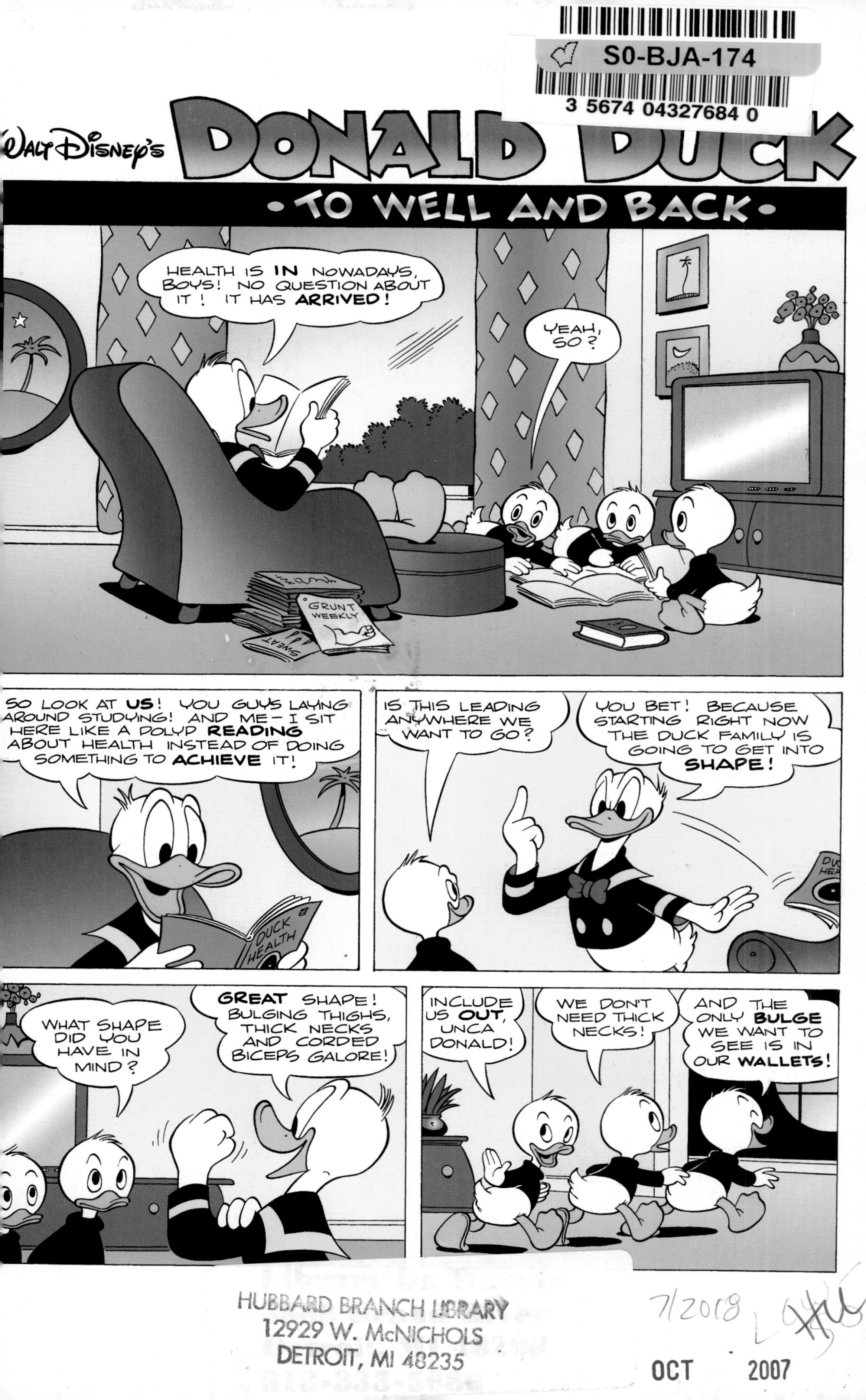
HEALTH IS IN NOWADAYS, BOYS! NO QUESTION ABOUT IT! IT HAS ARRIVED!
YEAH, SO?
GRUNT WEEKLY
SWEAT
SO LOOK AT US! YOU GUYS LAYING AROUND STUDYING! AND ME—I SIT HERE LIKE A POLYP READING ABOUT HEALTH INSTEAD OF DOING SOMETHING TO ACHIEVE IT!
DUCK HEALTH
IS THIS LEADING ANYWHERE WE WANT TO GO?
YOU BET! BECAUSE STARTING RIGHT NOW THE DUCK FAMILY IS GOING TO GET INTO SHAPE!
WHAT SHAPE DID YOU HAVE IN MIND?
GREAT SHAPE! BULGING THIGHS, THICK NECKS AND CORDED BICEPS GALORE!
INCLUDE US OUT, UNCA DONALD!
WE DON'T NEED THICK NECKS!
AND THE ONLY BULGE WE WANT TO SEE IS IN OUR WALLETS!

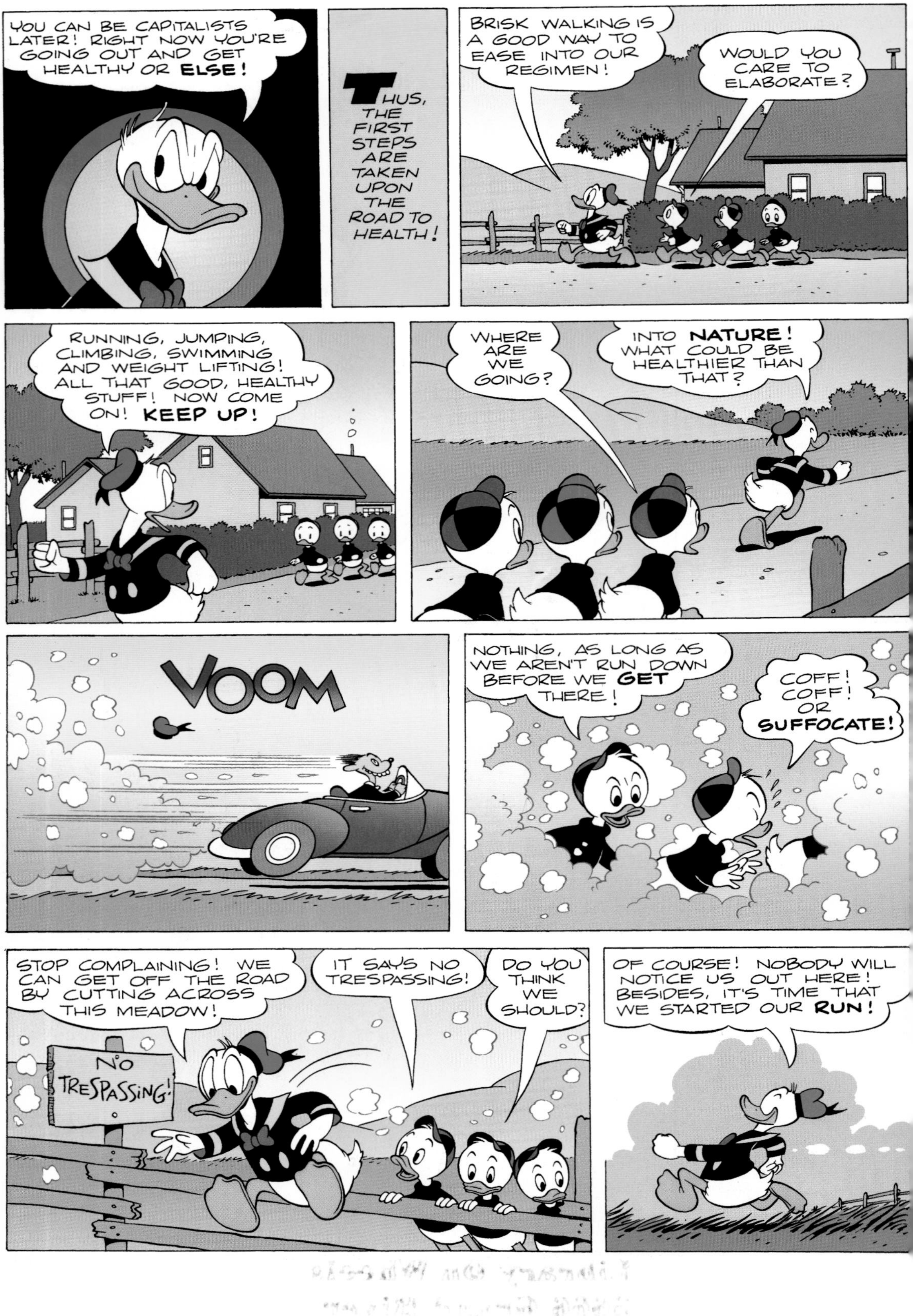
YOU CAN BE CAPITALISTS LATER! RIGHT NOW YOU'RE GOING OUT AND GET HEALTHY OR ELSE!
THUS, THE FIRST STEPS ARE TAKEN UPON THE ROAD TO HEALTH!
BRISK WALKING IS A GOOD WAY TO EASE INTO OUR REGIMEN!
WOULD YOU CARE TO ELABORATE?
RUNNING, JUMPING, CLIMBING, SWIMMING AND WEIGHT LIFTING! ALL THAT GOOD, HEALTHY STUFF! NOW COME ON! KEEP UP!
WHERE ARE WE GOING?
INTO NATURE! WHAT COULD BE HEALTHIER THAN THAT?
VOOM
NOTHING, AS LONG AS WE AREN'T RUN DOWN BEFORE WE GET THERE!
COFF! COFF! OR SUFFOCATE!
STOP COMPLAINING! WE CAN GET OFF THE ROAD BY CUTTING ACROSS THIS MEADOW!
NO TRESPASSING!
IT SAYS NO TRESPASSING!
DO YOU THINK WE SHOULD?
OF COURSE! NOBODY WILL NOTICE US OUT HERE! BESIDES, IT'S TIME THAT WE STARTED OUR RUN!

3567404327(4?)840

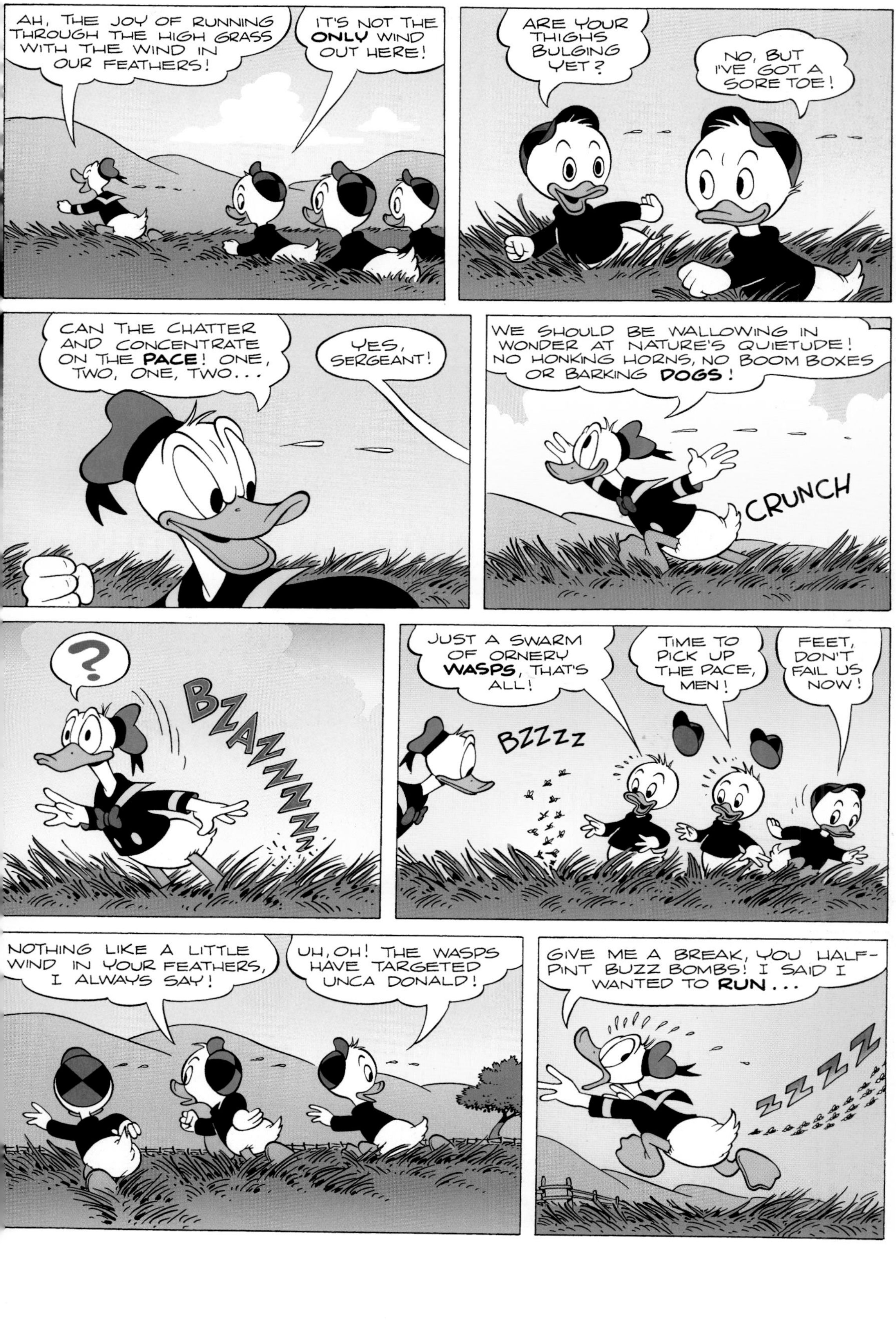
AH, THE JOY OF RUNNING THROUGH THE HIGH GRASS WITH THE WIND IN OUR FEATHERS!
IT'S NOT THE ONLY WIND OUT HERE!
ARE YOUR THIGHS BULGING YET?
NO, BUT I'VE GOT A SORE TOE!
CAN THE CHATTER AND CONCENTRATE ON THE PACE! ONE, TWO, ONE, TWO...
YES, SERGEANT!
WE SHOULD BE WALLOWING IN WONDER AT NATURE'S QUIETUDE! NO HONKING HORNS, NO BOOM BOXES OR BARKING DOGS!
CRUNCH
?
BZZZZZZZZ
JUST A SWARM OF ORNERY WASPS, THAT'S ALL!
TIME TO PICK UP THE PACE, MEN!
FEET, DON'T FAIL US NOW!
BZZZz
NOTHING LIKE A LITTLE WIND IN YOUR FEATHERS, I ALWAYS SAY!
UH, OH! THE WASPS HAVE TARGETED UNCA DONALD!
GIVE ME A BREAK, YOU HALF-PINT BUZZ BOMBS! I SAID I WANTED TO RUN...
ZZZZ

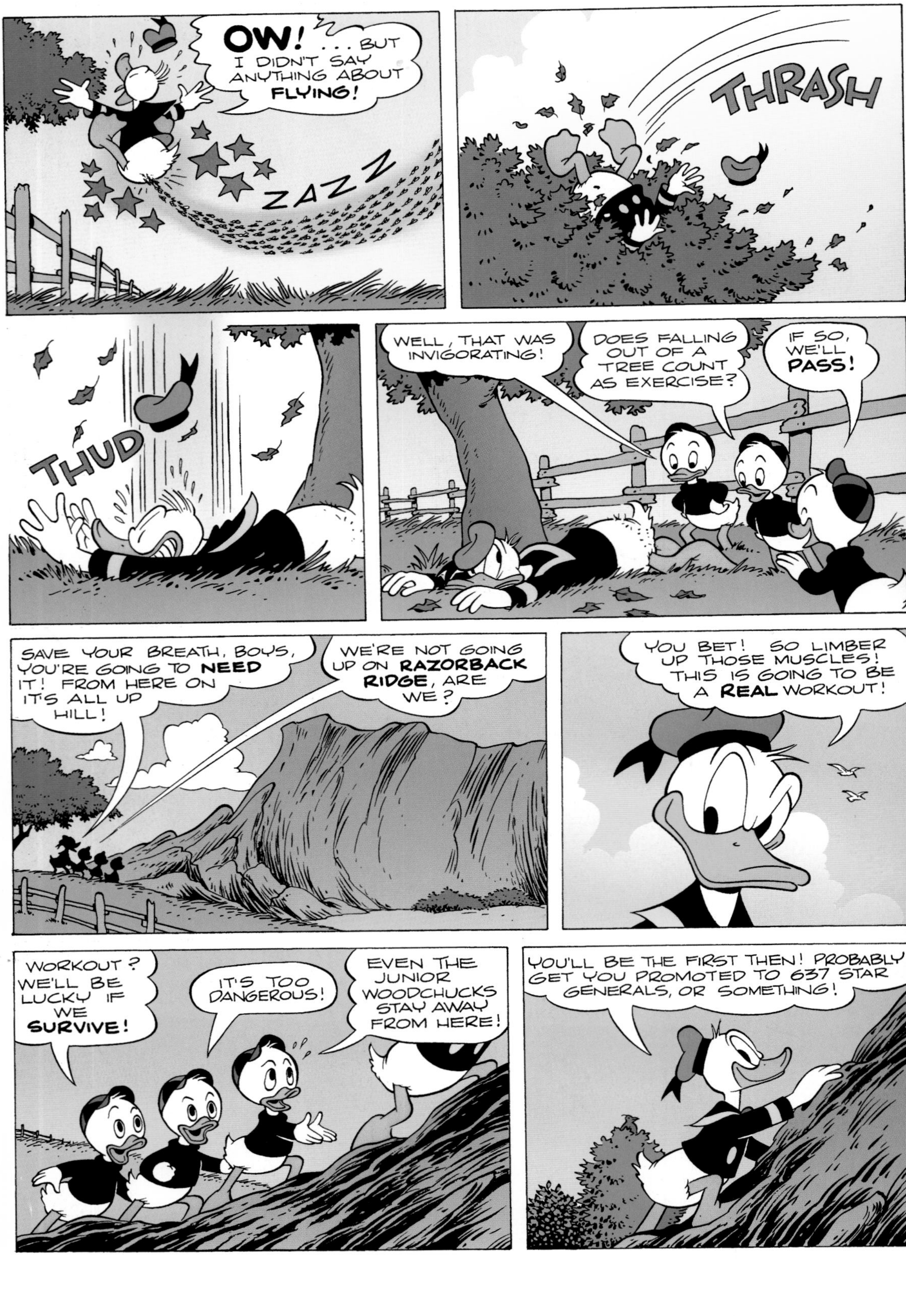
OW! ... BUT I DIDN'T SAY ANYTHING ABOUT FLYING!
ZAZZ
THRASH
THUD
WELL, THAT WAS INVIGORATING!
DOES FALLING OUT OF A TREE COUNT AS EXERCISE?
IF SO, WE'LL PASS!
SAVE YOUR BREATH, BOYS, YOU'RE GOING TO NEED IT! FROM HERE ON IT'S ALL UP HILL!
WE'RE NOT GOING UP ON RAZORBACK RIDGE, ARE WE?
YOU BET! SO LIMBER UP THOSE MUSCLES! THIS IS GOING TO BE A REAL WORKOUT!
WORKOUT? WE'LL BE LUCKY IF WE SURVIVE!
IT'S TOO DANGEROUS!
EVEN THE JUNIOR WOODCHUCKS STAY AWAY FROM HERE!
YOU'LL BE THE FIRST THEN! PROBABLY GET YOU PROMOTED TO 637 STAR GENERALS, OR SOMETHING!

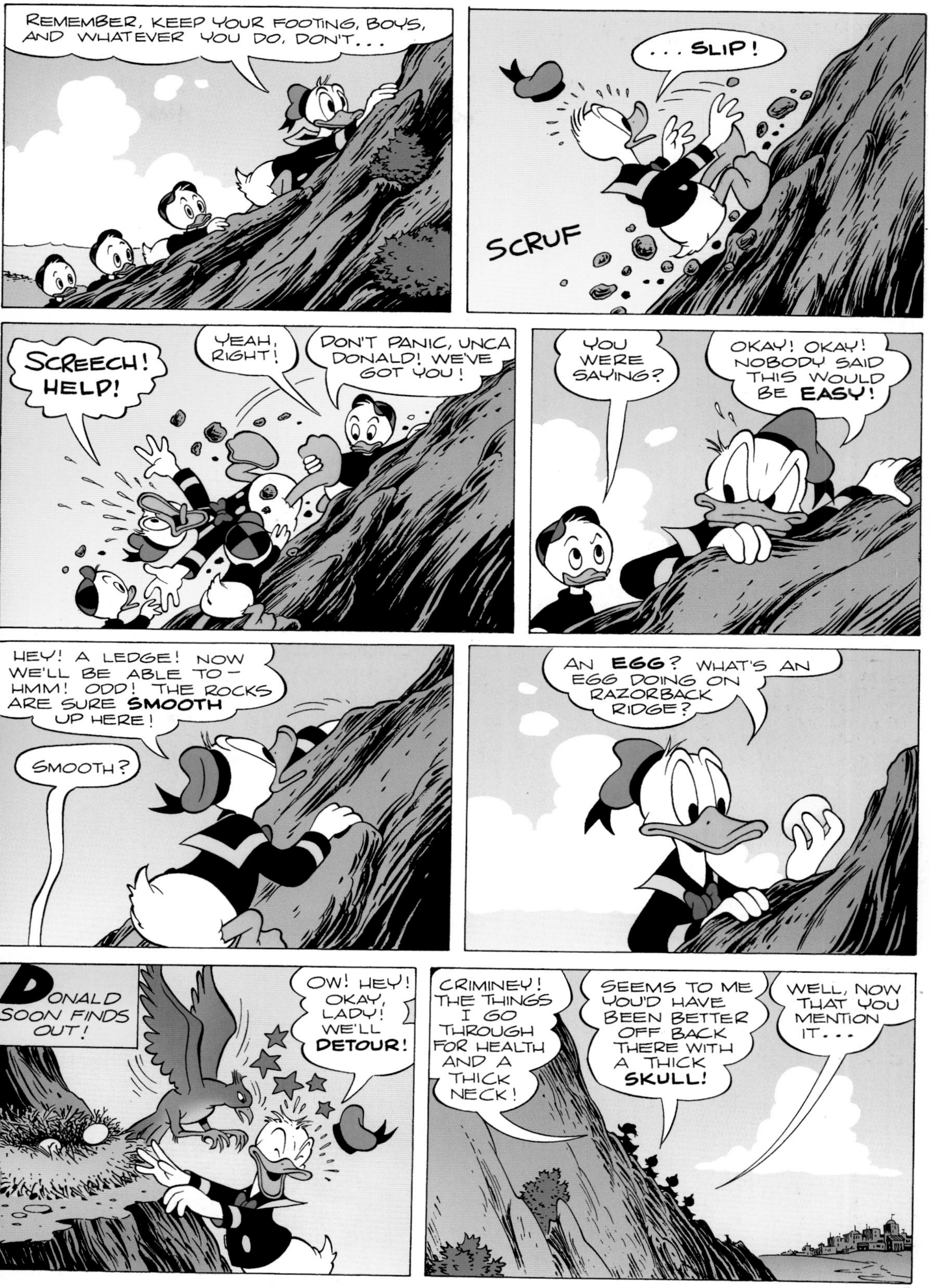
REMEMBER, KEEP YOUR FOOTING, BOYS, AND WHATEVER YOU DO, DON'T...
...SLIP!
SCRUF
SCREECH! HELP!
YEAH, RIGHT!
DON'T PANIC, UNCA DONALD! WE'VE GOT YOU!
YOU WERE SAYING?
OKAY! OKAY! NOBODY SAID THIS WOULD BE EASY!
HEY! A LEDGE! NOW WE'LL BE ABLE TO— HMM! ODD! THE ROCKS ARE SURE SMOOTH UP HERE!
SMOOTH?
AN EGG? WHAT'S AN EGG DOING ON RAZORBACK RIDGE?
DONALD SOON FINDS OUT!
OW! HEY! OKAY, LADY! WE'LL DETOUR!
CRIMINEY! THE THINGS I GO THROUGH FOR HEALTH AND A THICK NECK!
SEEMS TO ME YOU'D HAVE BEEN BETTER OFF BACK THERE WITH A THICK SKULL!
WELL, NOW THAT YOU MENTION IT...

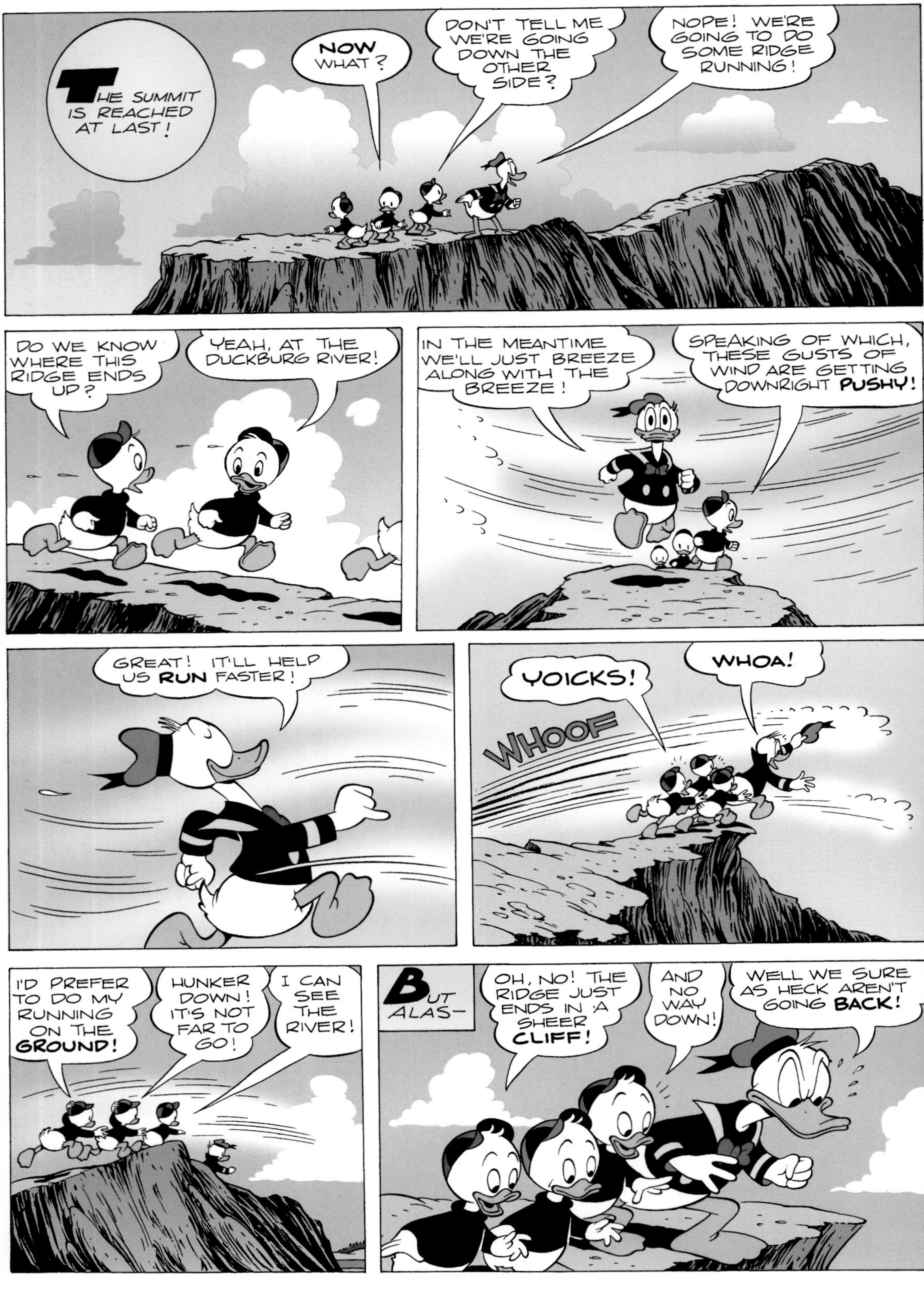
THE SUMMIT IS REACHED AT LAST!
NOW WHAT?
DON'T TELL ME WE'RE GOING DOWN THE OTHER SIDE?
NOPE! WE'RE GOING TO DO SOME RIDGE RUNNING!
DO WE KNOW WHERE THIS RIDGE ENDS UP?
YEAH, AT THE DUCKBURG RIVER!
IN THE MEANTIME WE'LL JUST BREEZE ALONG WITH THE BREEZE!
SPEAKING OF WHICH, THESE GUSTS OF WIND ARE GETTING DOWNRIGHT PUSHY!
GREAT! IT'LL HELP US RUN FASTER!
WHOOF
YOICKS!
WHOA!
I'D PREFER TO DO MY RUNNING ON THE GROUND!
HUNKER DOWN! IT'S NOT FAR TO GO!
I CAN SEE THE RIVER!
BUT ALAS—
OH, NO! THE RIDGE JUST ENDS IN A SHEER CLIFF!
AND NO WAY DOWN!
WELL WE SURE AS HECK AREN'T GOING BACK!

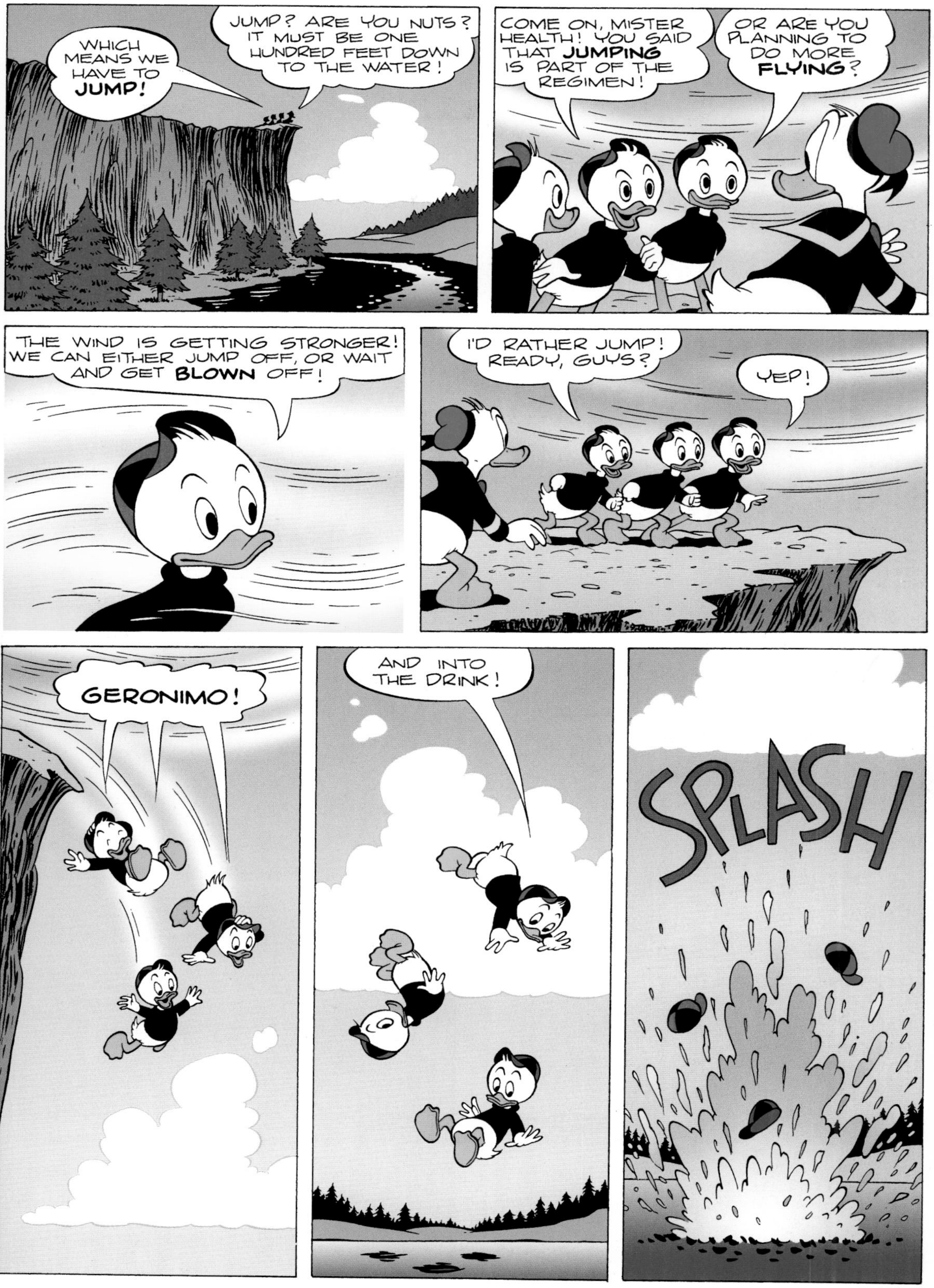
WHICH MEANS WE HAVE TO JUMP!
JUMP? ARE YOU NUTS? IT MUST BE ONE HUNDRED FEET DOWN TO THE WATER!
COME ON, MISTER HEALTH! YOU SAID THAT JUMPING IS PART OF THE REGIMEN!
OR ARE YOU PLANNING TO DO MORE FLYING?
THE WIND IS GETTING STRONGER! WE CAN EITHER JUMP OFF, OR WAIT AND GET BLOWN OFF!
I'D RATHER JUMP! READY, GUYS?
YEP!
GERONIMO!
AND INTO THE DRINK!
SPLASH

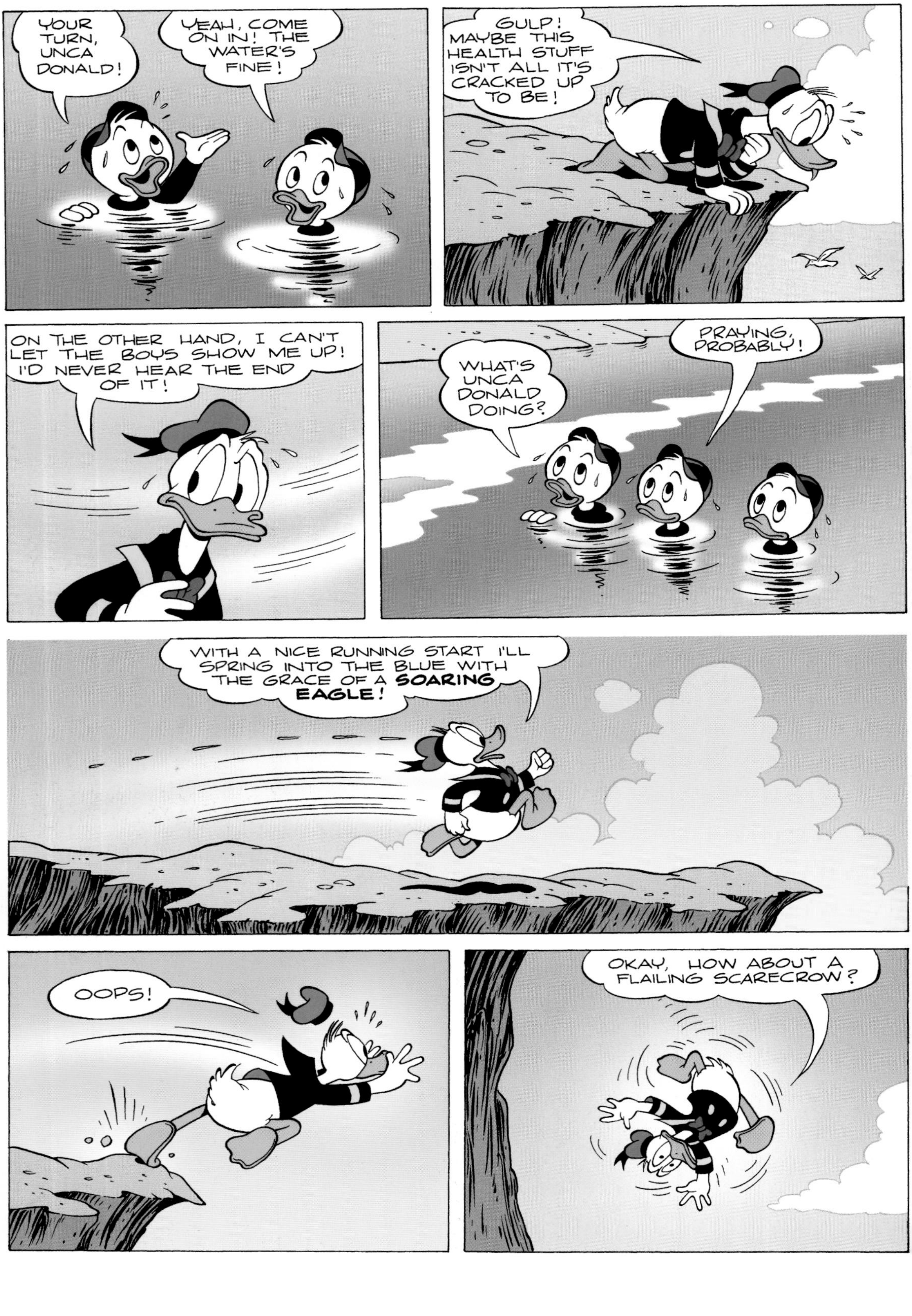
YOUR TURN, UNCA DONALD!
YEAH, COME ON IN! THE WATER'S FINE!
GULP! MAYBE THIS HEALTH STUFF ISN'T ALL IT'S CRACKED UP TO BE!
ON THE OTHER HAND, I CAN'T LET THE BOYS SHOW ME UP! I'D NEVER HEAR THE END OF IT!
WHAT'S UNCA DONALD DOING?
PRAYING, PROBABLY!
WITH A NICE RUNNING START I'LL SPRING INTO THE BLUE WITH THE GRACE OF A **SOARING EAGLE**!
OOPS!
OKAY, HOW ABOUT A FLAILING SCARECROW?

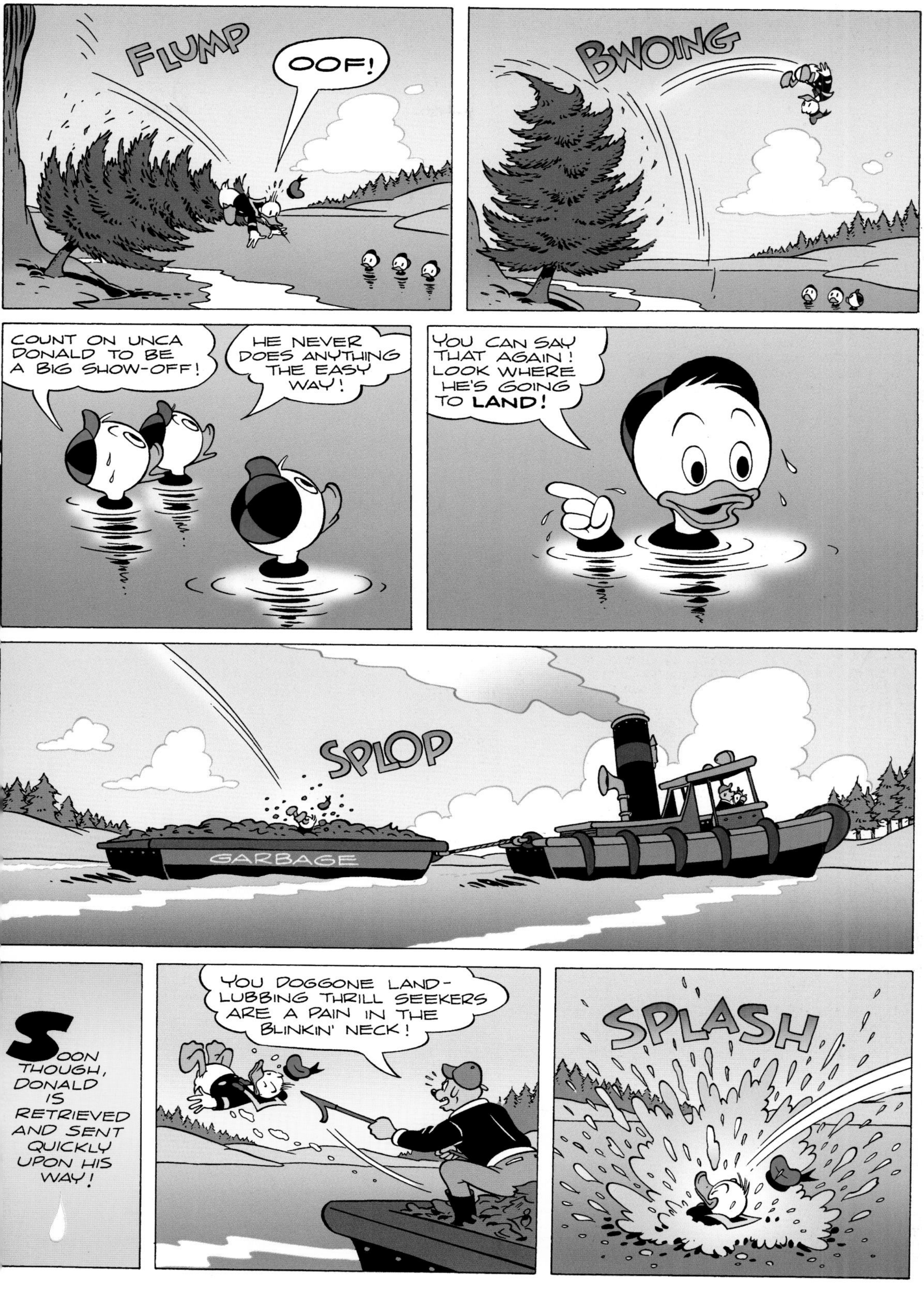
FLUMP
OOF!
BWOING
COUNT ON UNCA DONALD TO BE A BIG SHOW-OFF!
HE NEVER DOES ANYTHING THE EASY WAY!
YOU CAN SAY THAT AGAIN! LOOK WHERE HE'S GOING TO LAND!
SPLOP
GARBAGE
SOON THOUGH, DONALD IS RETRIEVED AND SENT QUICKLY UPON HIS WAY!
YOU DOGGONE LAND-LUBBING THRILL SEEKERS ARE A PAIN IN THE BLINKIN' NECK!
SPLASH

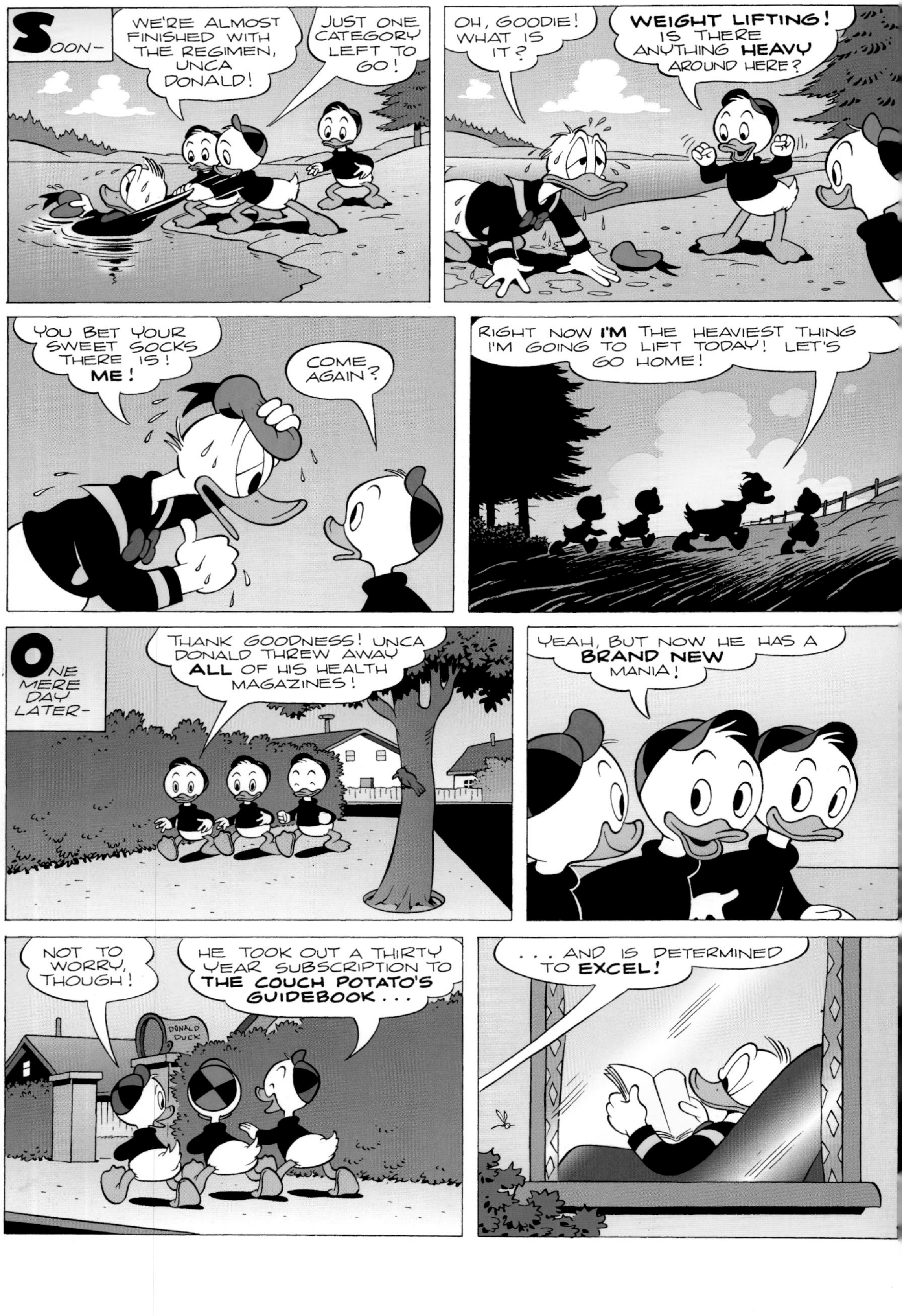

SOON-
WE'RE ALMOST FINISHED WITH THE REGIMEN, UNCA DONALD!
JUST ONE CATEGORY LEFT TO GO!
OH, GOODIE! WHAT IS IT?
WEIGHT LIFTING! IS THERE ANYTHING HEAVY AROUND HERE?
YOU BET YOUR SWEET SOCKS THERE IS! ME!
COME AGAIN?
RIGHT NOW I'M THE HEAVIEST THING I'M GOING TO LIFT TODAY! LET'S GO HOME!
ONE MERE DAY LATER-
THANK GOODNESS! UNCA DONALD THREW AWAY ALL OF HIS HEALTH MAGAZINES!
YEAH, BUT NOW HE HAS A BRAND NEW MANIA!
NOT TO WORRY, THOUGH!
HE TOOK OUT A THIRTY YEAR SUBSCRIPTION TO THE COUCH POTATO'S GUIDEBOOK...
DONALD DUCK
...AND IS DETERMINED TO EXCEL!

Walt Disney's

MICKEY MOUSE in VACATION BRAKE

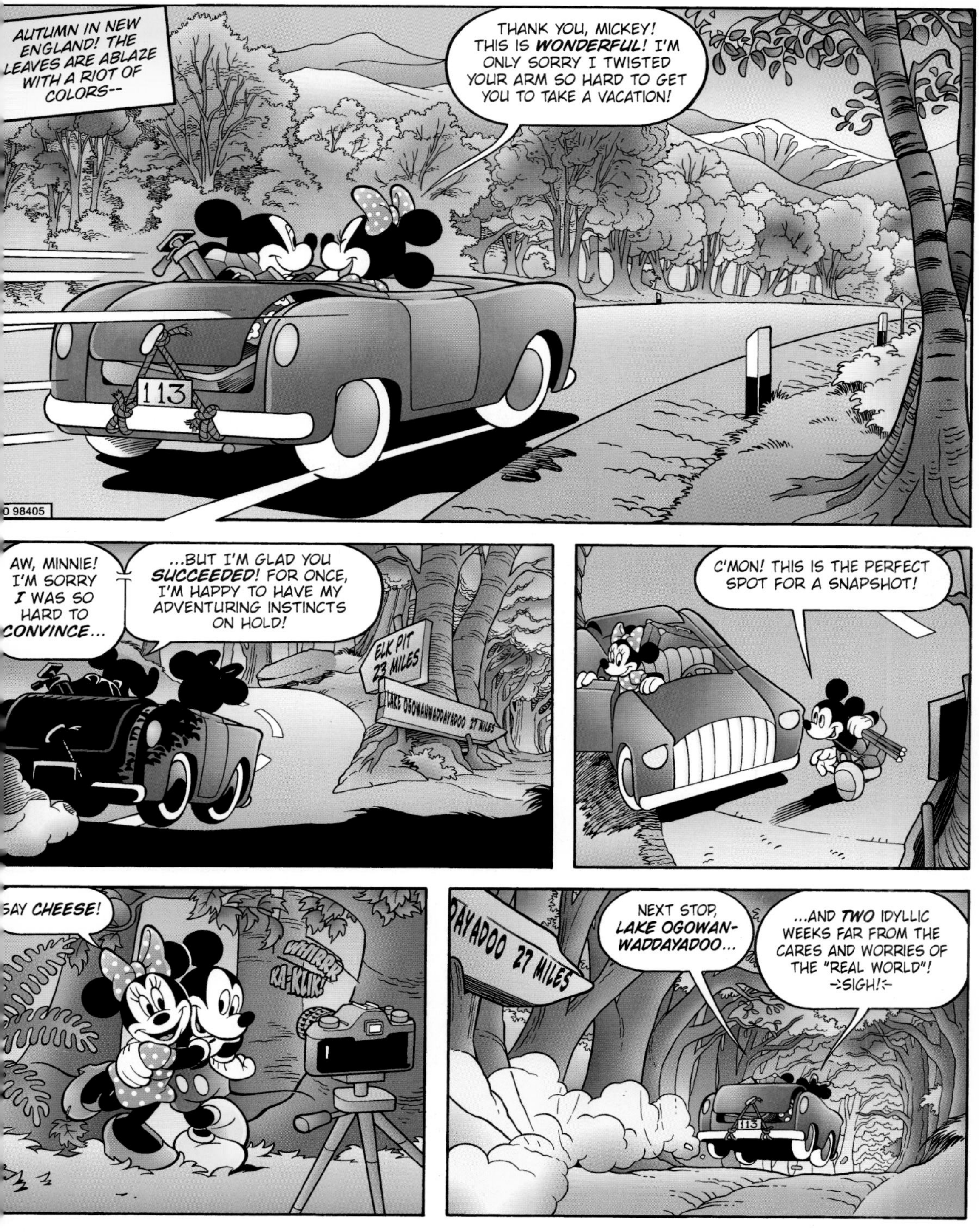

AUTUMN IN NEW ENGLAND! THE LEAVES ARE ABLAZE WITH A RIOT OF COLORS--
THANK YOU, MICKEY! THIS IS **WONDERFUL!** I'M ONLY SORRY I TWISTED YOUR ARM SO HARD TO GET YOU TO TAKE A VACATION!
113
D 98405
AW, MINNIE! I'M SORRY ***I*** WAS SO HARD TO ***CONVINCE...***
...BUT I'M GLAD YOU ***SUCCEEDED!*** FOR ONCE, I'M HAPPY TO HAVE MY ADVENTURING INSTINCTS ON HOLD!
ELK PIT 23 MILES
LAKE OGOWANWADDAYADOO 27 MILES
C'MON! THIS IS THE PERFECT SPOT FOR A SNAPSHOT!
SAY ***CHEESE!***
WHIRRR
KA-KLIK!
DAYADOO 27 MILES
NEXT STOP, ***LAKE OGOWAN-WADDAYADOO...***
...AND ***TWO*** IDYLLIC WEEKS FAR FROM THE CARES AND WORRIES OF THE "REAL WORLD"! -SIGH!-
113

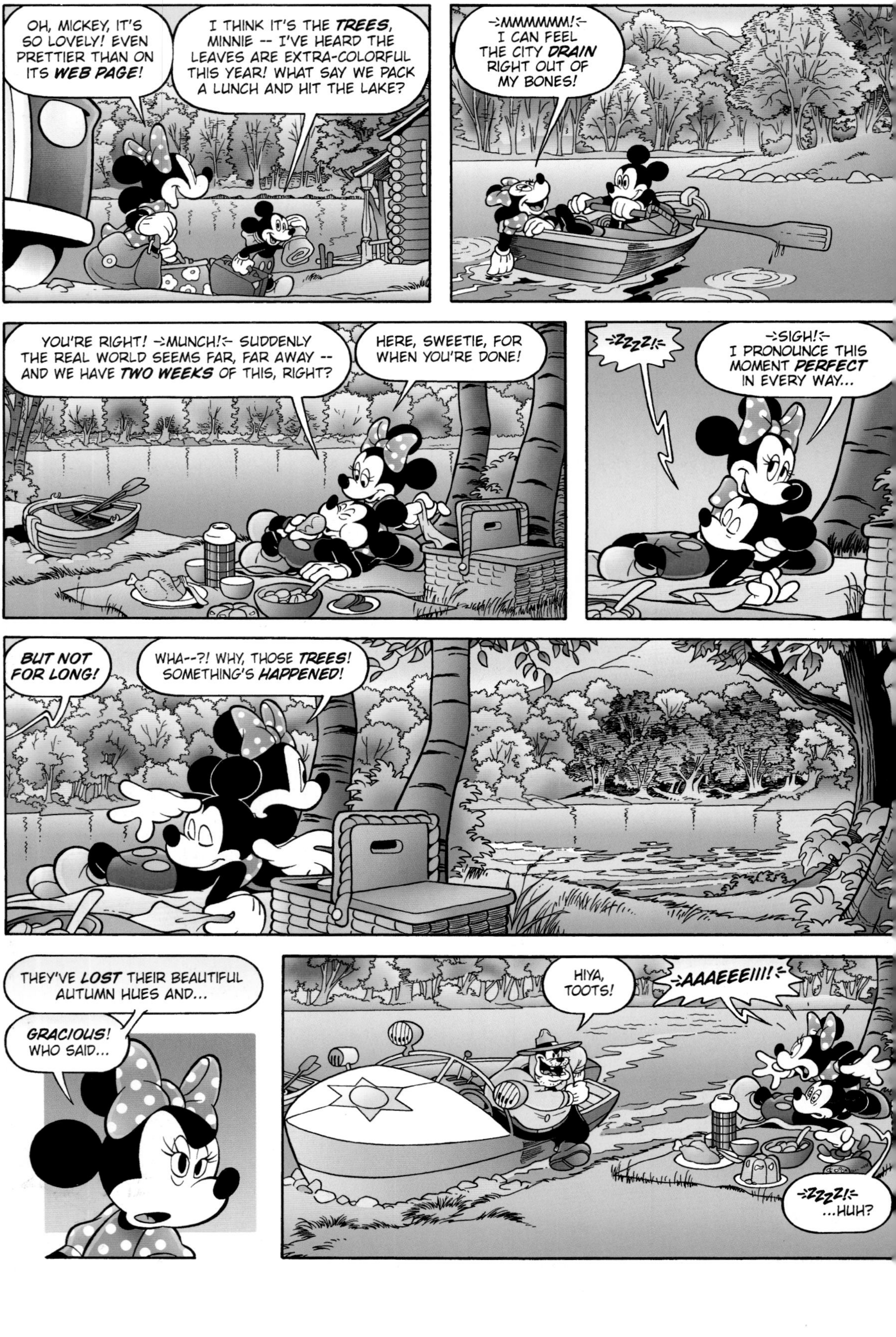
OH, MICKEY, IT'S SO LOVELY! EVEN PRETTIER THAN ON ITS WEB PAGE!
I THINK IT'S THE TREES, MINNIE -- I'VE HEARD THE LEAVES ARE EXTRA-COLORFUL THIS YEAR! WHAT SAY WE PACK A LUNCH AND HIT THE LAKE?
-MMMMMM!- I CAN FEEL THE CITY DRAIN RIGHT OUT OF MY BONES!
YOU'RE RIGHT! -MUNCH!- SUDDENLY THE REAL WORLD SEEMS FAR, FAR AWAY -- AND WE HAVE TWO WEEKS OF THIS, RIGHT?
HERE, SWEETIE, FOR WHEN YOU'RE DONE!
-ZZZZ!-
-SIGH!- I PRONOUNCE THIS MOMENT PERFECT IN EVERY WAY...
BUT NOT FOR LONG!
WHA--?! WHY, THOSE TREES! SOMETHING'S HAPPENED!
THEY'VE LOST THEIR BEAUTIFUL AUTUMN HUES AND...
GRACIOUS! WHO SAID...
HIYA, TOOTS!
-AAAEEEIIII!-
-ZZZZ!- ...HUH?

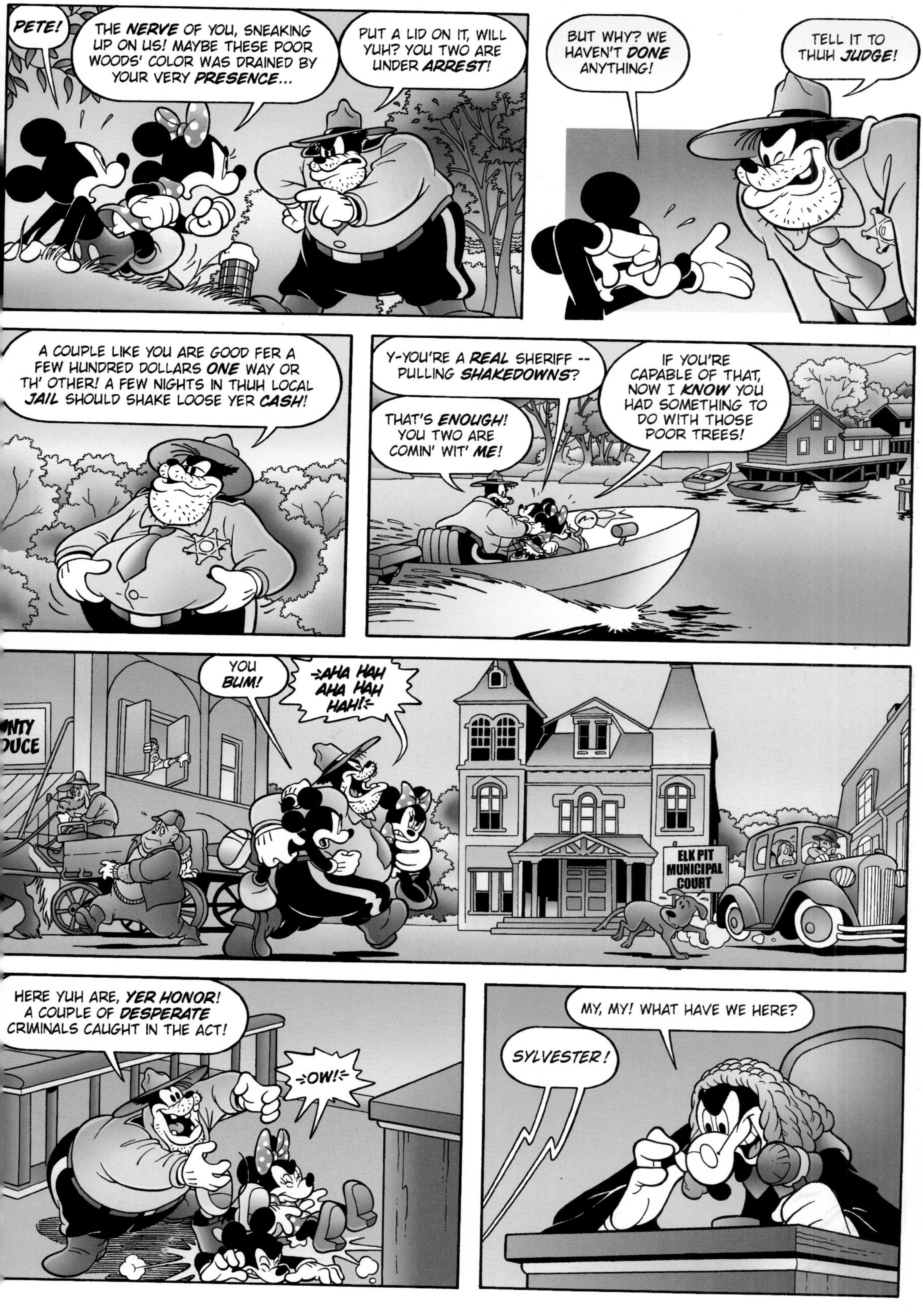
PETE!
THE NERVE OF YOU, SNEAKING UP ON US! MAYBE THESE POOR WOODS' COLOR WAS DRAINED BY YOUR VERY PRESENCE...
PUT A LID ON IT, WILL YUH? YOU TWO ARE UNDER ARREST!
BUT WHY? WE HAVEN'T DONE ANYTHING!
TELL IT TO THUH JUDGE!
A COUPLE LIKE YOU ARE GOOD FER A FEW HUNDRED DOLLARS ONE WAY OR TH' OTHER! A FEW NIGHTS IN THUH LOCAL JAIL SHOULD SHAKE LOOSE YER CASH!
Y-YOU'RE A REAL SHERIFF -- PULLING SHAKEDOWNS?
THAT'S ENOUGH! YOU TWO ARE COMIN' WIT' ME!
IF YOU'RE CAPABLE OF THAT, NOW I KNOW YOU HAD SOMETHING TO DO WITH THOSE POOR TREES!
YOU BUM!
AHA HAH AHA HAH HAH!
ELK PIT MUNICIPAL COURT
HERE YUH ARE, YER HONOR! A COUPLE OF DESPERATE CRIMINALS CAUGHT IN THE ACT!
OW!
MY, MY! WHAT HAVE WE HERE?
SYLVESTER!

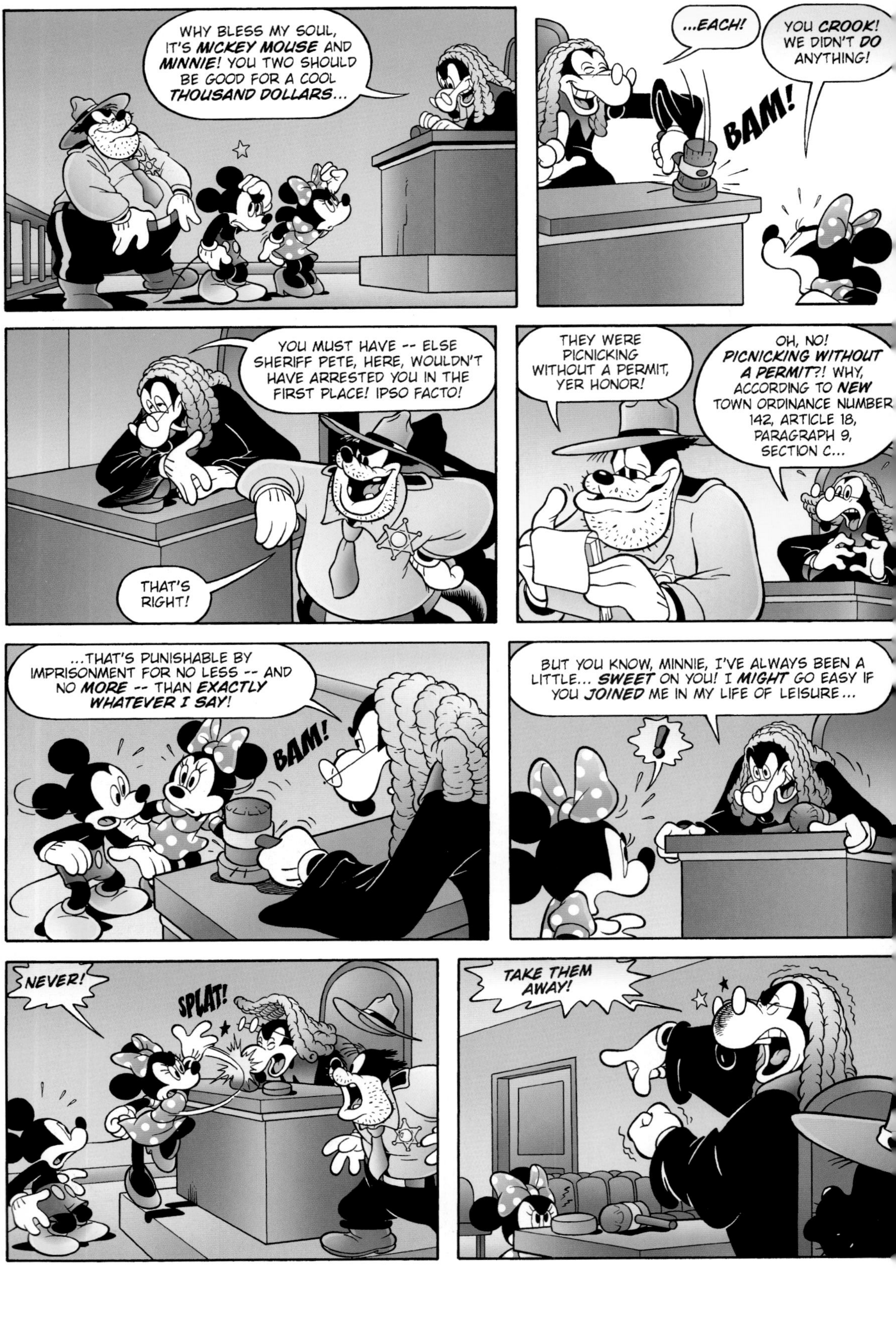
WHY BLESS MY SOUL, IT'S MICKEY MOUSE AND MINNIE! YOU TWO SHOULD BE GOOD FOR A COOL THOUSAND DOLLARS...
...EACH!
YOU CROOK! WE DIDN'T DO ANYTHING!
BAM!
YOU MUST HAVE -- ELSE SHERIFF PETE, HERE, WOULDN'T HAVE ARRESTED YOU IN THE FIRST PLACE! IPSO FACTO!
THAT'S RIGHT!
THEY WERE PICNICKING WITHOUT A PERMIT, YER HONOR!
OH, NO! PICNICKING WITHOUT A PERMIT?! WHY, ACCORDING TO NEW TOWN ORDINANCE NUMBER 142, ARTICLE 18, PARAGRAPH 9, SECTION C...
...THAT'S PUNISHABLE BY IMPRISONMENT FOR NO LESS -- AND NO MORE -- THAN EXACTLY WHATEVER I SAY!
BAM!
BUT YOU KNOW, MINNIE, I'VE ALWAYS BEEN A LITTLE... SWEET ON YOU! I MIGHT GO EASY IF YOU JOINED ME IN MY LIFE OF LEISURE...
NEVER!
SPLAT!
TAKE THEM AWAY!

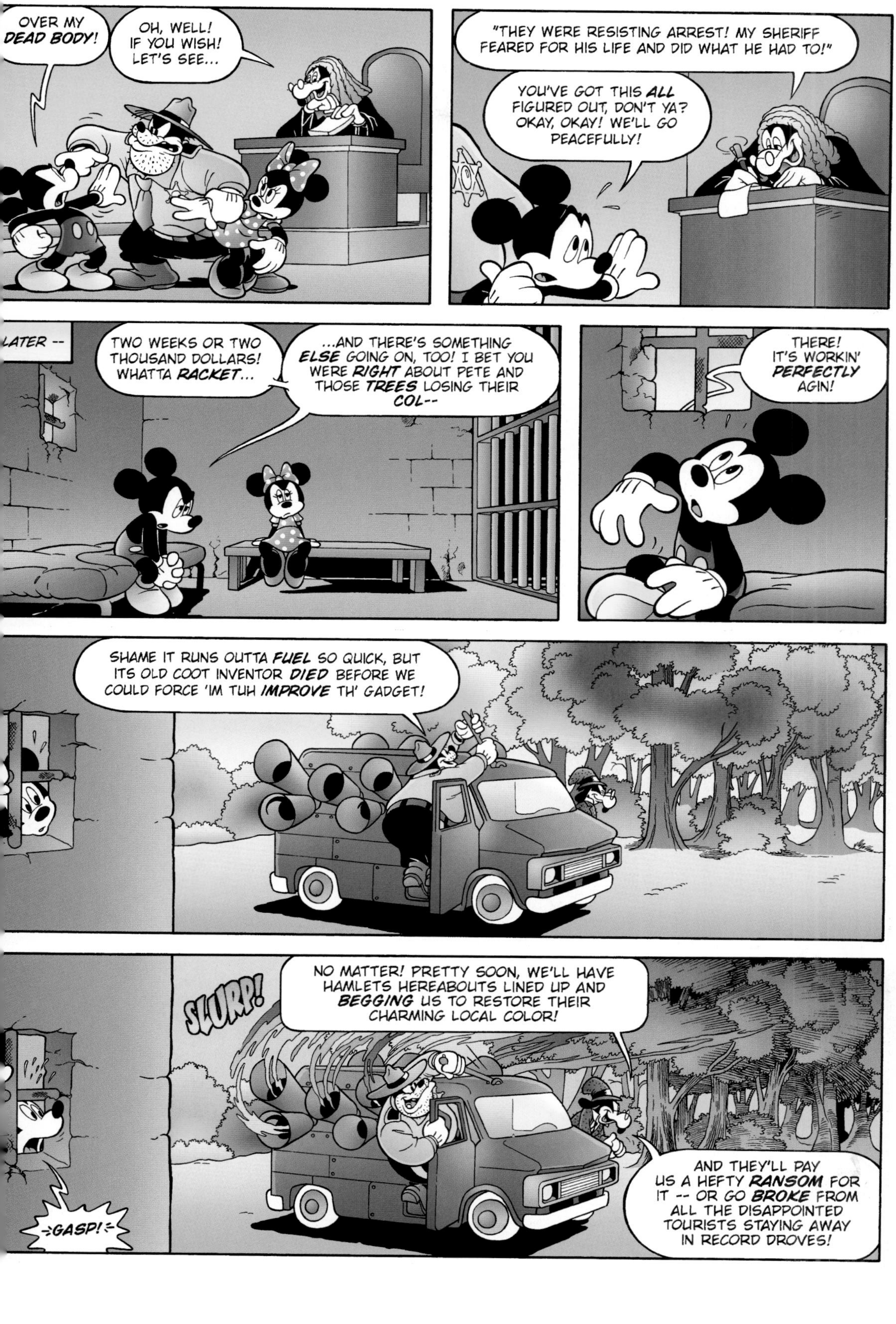
OVER MY DEAD BODY!
OH, WELL! IF YOU WISH! LET'S SEE...
"THEY WERE RESISTING ARREST! MY SHERIFF FEARED FOR HIS LIFE AND DID WHAT HE HAD TO!"
YOU'VE GOT THIS ALL FIGURED OUT, DON'T YA? OKAY, OKAY! WE'LL GO PEACEFULLY!
LATER --
TWO WEEKS OR TWO THOUSAND DOLLARS! WHATTA RACKET...
...AND THERE'S SOMETHING ELSE GOING ON, TOO! I BET YOU WERE RIGHT ABOUT PETE AND THOSE TREES LOSING THEIR COL--
THERE! IT'S WORKIN' PERFECTLY AGIN!
SHAME IT RUNS OUTTA FUEL SO QUICK, BUT ITS OLD COOT INVENTOR DIED BEFORE WE COULD FORCE 'IM TUH IMPROVE TH' GADGET!
SLURP!
NO MATTER! PRETTY SOON, WE'LL HAVE HAMLETS HEREABOUTS LINED UP AND BEGGING US TO RESTORE THEIR CHARMING LOCAL COLOR!
AND THEY'LL PAY US A HEFTY RANSOM FOR IT -- OR GO BROKE FROM ALL THE DISAPPOINTED TOURISTS STAYING AWAY IN RECORD DROVES!
GASP!

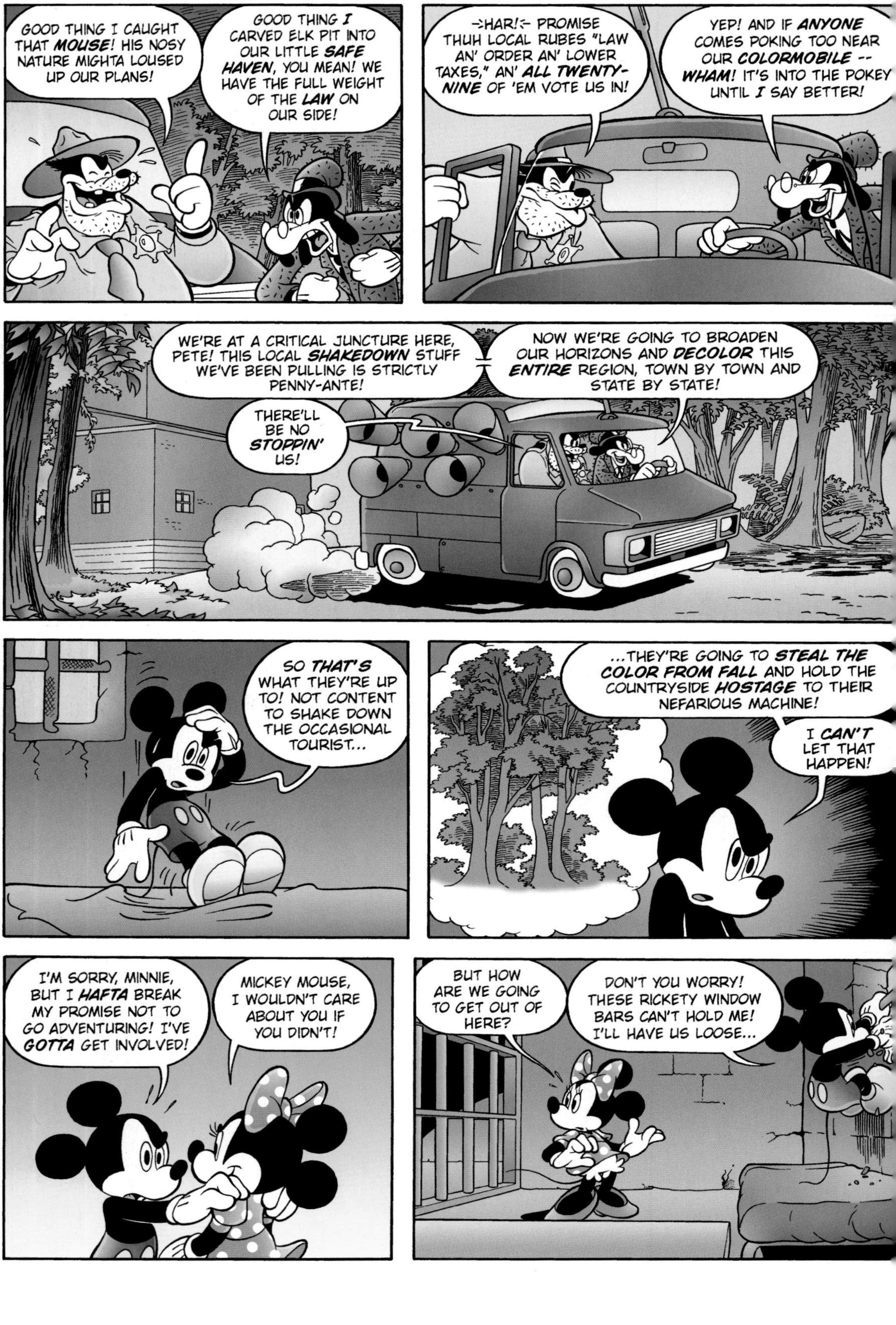
GOOD THING I CAUGHT THAT MOUSE! HIS NOSY NATURE MIGHTA LOUSED UP OUR PLANS!
GOOD THING I CARVED ELK PIT INTO OUR LITTLE SAFE HAVEN, YOU MEAN! WE HAVE THE FULL WEIGHT OF THE LAW ON OUR SIDE!
HAR! PROMISE THUH LOCAL RUBES "LAW AN' ORDER AN' LOWER TAXES," AN' ALL TWENTY-NINE OF 'EM VOTE US IN!
YEP! AND IF ANYONE COMES POKING TOO NEAR OUR COLORMOBILE -- WHAM! IT'S INTO THE POKEY UNTIL I SAY BETTER!
WE'RE AT A CRITICAL JUNCTURE HERE, PETE! THIS LOCAL SHAKEDOWN STUFF WE'VE BEEN PULLING IS STRICTLY PENNY-ANTE!
NOW WE'RE GOING TO BROADEN OUR HORIZONS AND DECOLOR THIS ENTIRE REGION, TOWN BY TOWN AND STATE BY STATE!
THERE'LL BE NO STOPPIN' US!
SO THAT'S WHAT THEY'RE UP TO! NOT CONTENT TO SHAKE DOWN THE OCCASIONAL TOURIST...
...THEY'RE GOING TO STEAL THE COLOR FROM FALL AND HOLD THE COUNTRYSIDE HOSTAGE TO THEIR NEFARIOUS MACHINE!
I CAN'T LET THAT HAPPEN!
I'M SORRY, MINNIE, BUT I HAFTA BREAK MY PROMISE NOT TO GO ADVENTURING! I'VE GOTTA GET INVOLVED!
MICKEY MOUSE, I WOULDN'T CARE ABOUT YOU IF YOU DIDN'T!
BUT HOW ARE WE GOING TO GET OUT OF HERE?
DON'T YOU WORRY! THESE RICKETY WINDOW BARS CAN'T HOLD ME! I'LL HAVE US LOOSE...

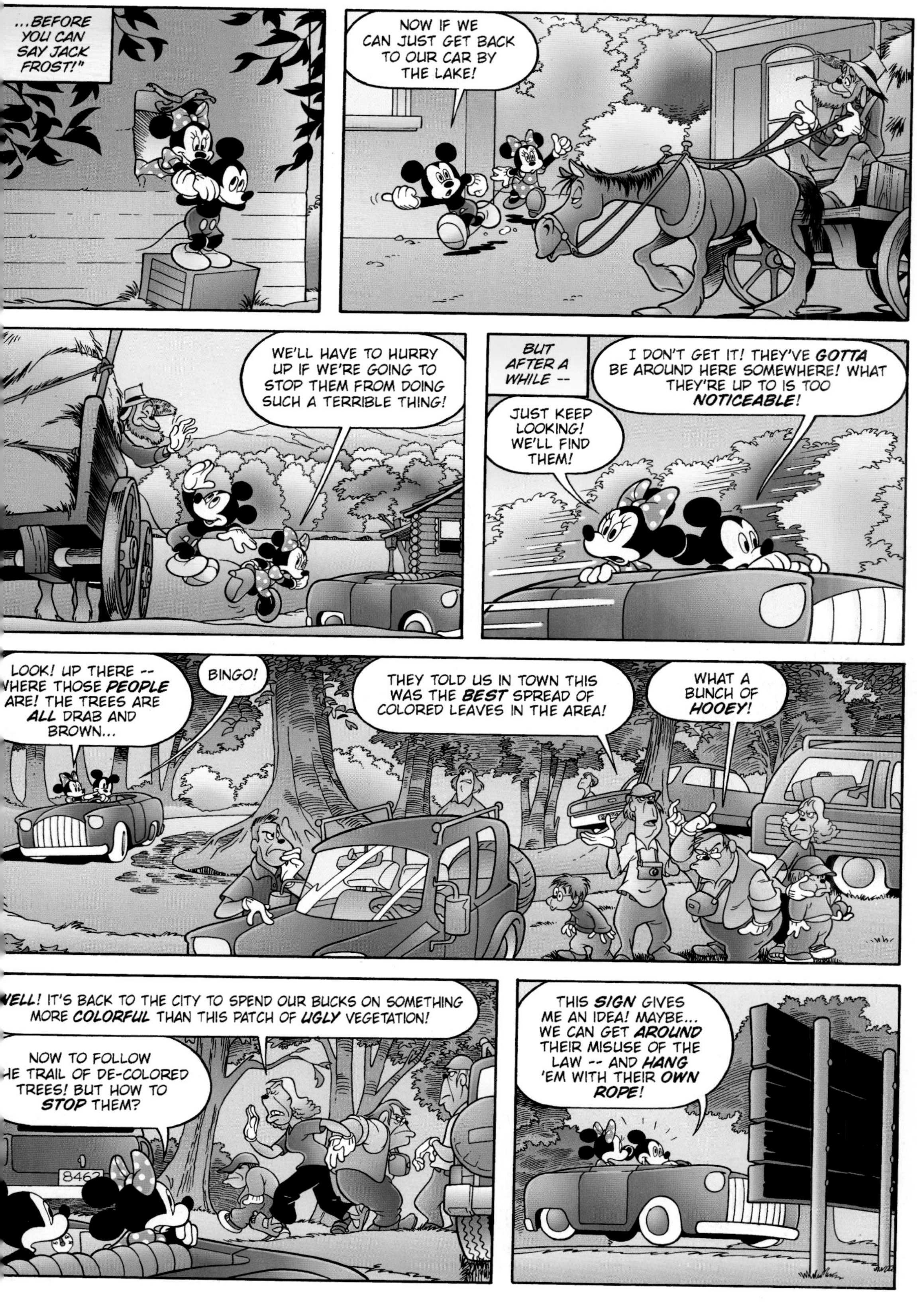

...BEFORE YOU CAN SAY JACK FROST!"
NOW IF WE CAN JUST GET BACK TO OUR CAR BY THE LAKE!
WE'LL HAVE TO HURRY UP IF WE'RE GOING TO STOP THEM FROM DOING SUCH A TERRIBLE THING!
BUT AFTER A WHILE --
I DON'T GET IT! THEY'VE GOTTA BE AROUND HERE SOMEWHERE! WHAT THEY'RE UP TO IS TOO NOTICEABLE!
JUST KEEP LOOKING! WE'LL FIND THEM!
LOOK! UP THERE -- WHERE THOSE PEOPLE ARE! THE TREES ARE ALL DRAB AND BROWN...
BINGO!
THEY TOLD US IN TOWN THIS WAS THE BEST SPREAD OF COLORED LEAVES IN THE AREA!
WHAT A BUNCH OF HOOEY!
WELL! IT'S BACK TO THE CITY TO SPEND OUR BUCKS ON SOMETHING MORE COLORFUL THAN THIS PATCH OF UGLY VEGETATION!
NOW TO FOLLOW THE TRAIL OF DE-COLORED TREES! BUT HOW TO STOP THEM?
THIS SIGN GIVES ME AN IDEA! MAYBE... WE CAN GET AROUND THEIR MISUSE OF THE LAW -- AND HANG 'EM WITH THEIR OWN ROPE!

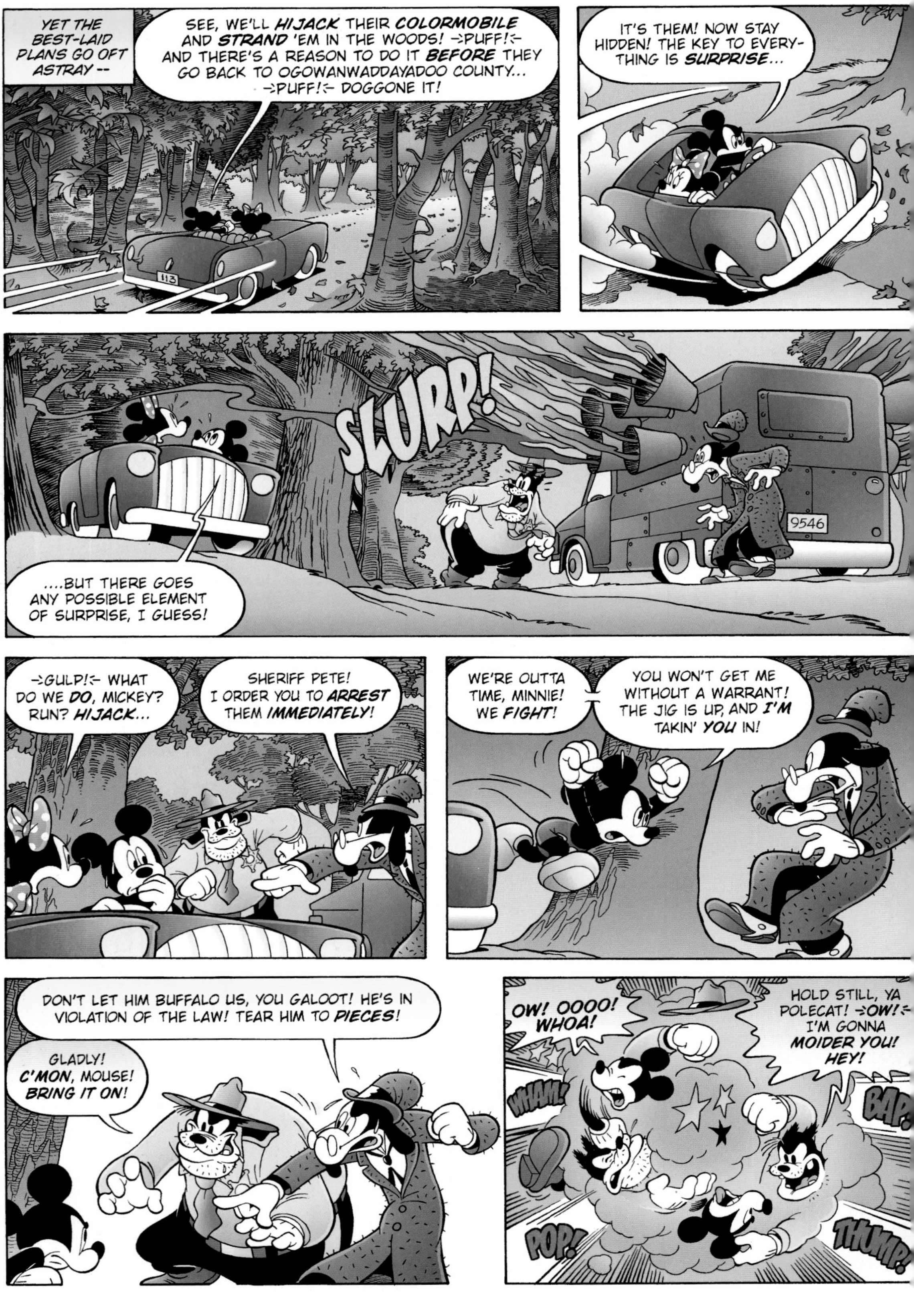
YET THE BEST-LAID PLANS GO OFT ASTRAY --
SEE, WE'LL HIJACK THEIR COLORMOBILE AND STRAND 'EM IN THE WOODS! ⇒PUFF!⇐ AND THERE'S A REASON TO DO IT BEFORE THEY GO BACK TO OGOWANWADDAYADOO COUNTY... ⇒PUFF!⇐ DOGGONE IT!
113
IT'S THEM! NOW STAY HIDDEN! THE KEY TO EVERYTHING IS SURPRISE...
SLURP!
9546
....BUT THERE GOES ANY POSSIBLE ELEMENT OF SURPRISE, I GUESS!
⇒GULP!⇐ WHAT DO WE DO, MICKEY? RUN? HIJACK...
SHERIFF PETE! I ORDER YOU TO ARREST THEM IMMEDIATELY!
WE'RE OUTTA TIME, MINNIE! WE FIGHT!
YOU WON'T GET ME WITHOUT A WARRANT! THE JIG IS UP, AND I'M TAKIN' YOU IN!
DON'T LET HIM BUFFALO US, YOU GALOOT! HE'S IN VIOLATION OF THE LAW! TEAR HIM TO PIECES!
GLADLY! C'MON, MOUSE! BRING IT ON!
OW! OOOO! WHOA!
HOLD STILL, YA POLECAT! ⇒OW!⇐ I'M GONNA MOIDER YOU! HEY!
WHAM!
BAP!
POP!
THUMP!

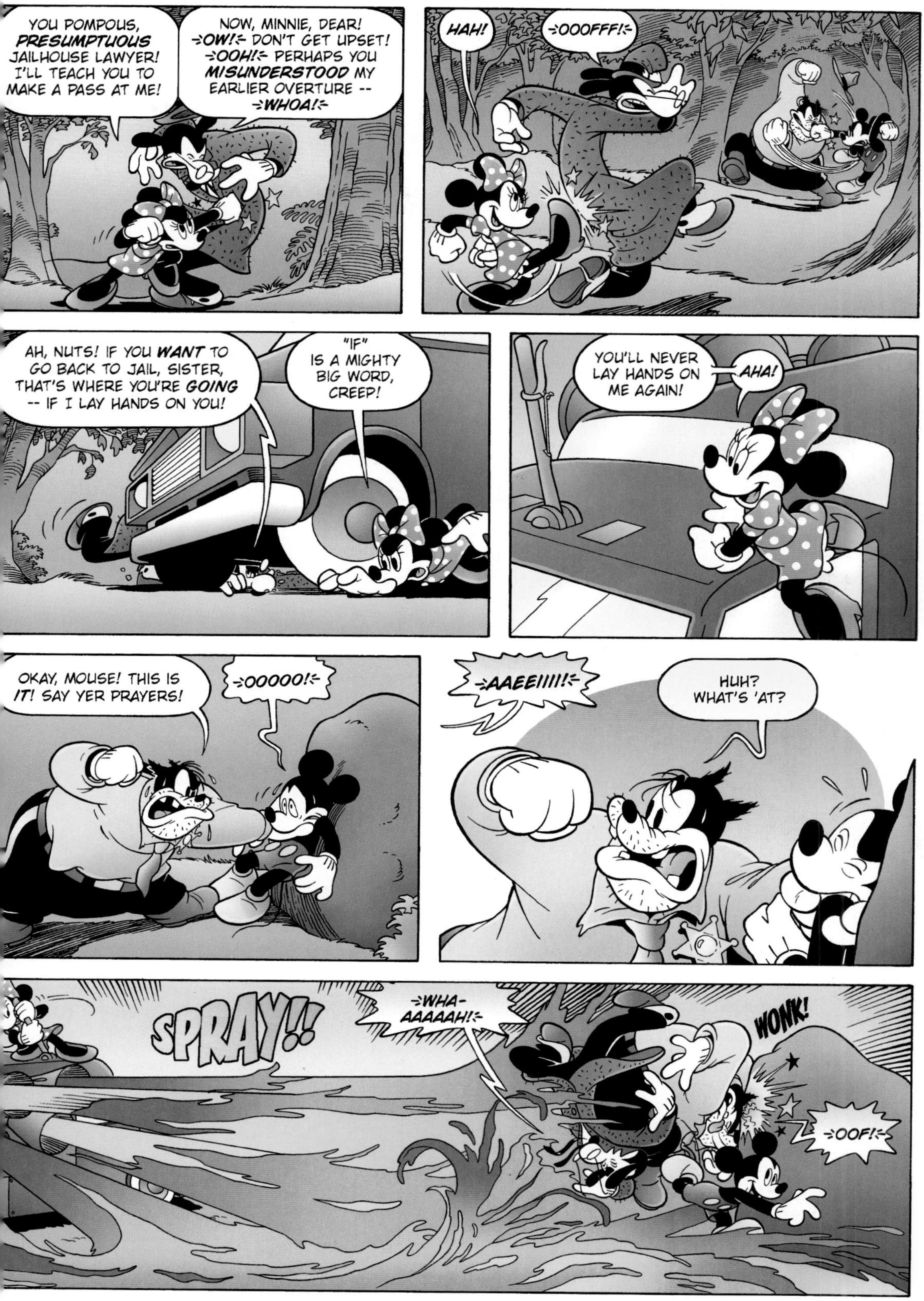
YOU POMPOUS, PRESUMPTUOUS JAILHOUSE LAWYER! I'LL TEACH YOU TO MAKE A PASS AT ME!
NOW, MINNIE, DEAR! -OW!- DON'T GET UPSET! -OOH!- PERHAPS YOU MISUNDERSTOOD MY EARLIER OVERTURE -- -WHOA!-
HAH!
-OOOFFF!-
AH, NUTS! IF YOU WANT TO GO BACK TO JAIL, SISTER, THAT'S WHERE YOU'RE GOING -- IF I LAY HANDS ON YOU!
"IF" IS A MIGHTY BIG WORD, CREEP!
YOU'LL NEVER LAY HANDS ON ME AGAIN!
AHA!
OKAY, MOUSE! THIS IS IT! SAY YER PRAYERS!
-OOOOO!-
-AAEE!!!!!-
HUH? WHAT'S 'AT?
SPRAY!!
-WHA-AAAAAH!-
WONK!
-OOF!-

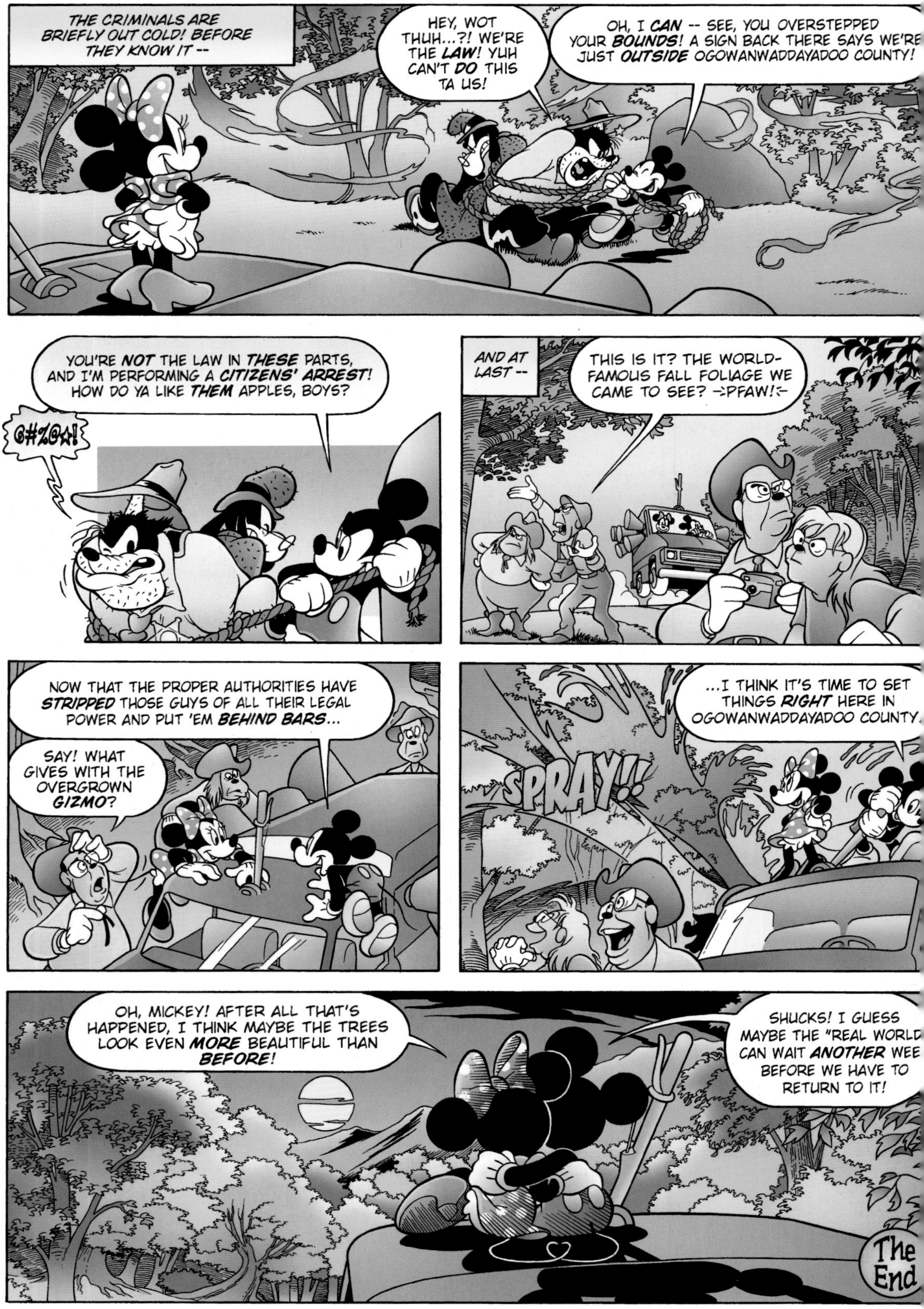
THE CRIMINALS ARE BRIEFLY OUT COLD! BEFORE THEY KNOW IT --
HEY, WOT THUH...?! WE'RE THE LAW! YUH CAN'T DO THIS TA US!
OH, I CAN -- SEE, YOU OVERSTEPPED YOUR BOUNDS! A SIGN BACK THERE SAYS WE'RE JUST OUTSIDE OGOWANWADDAYADOO COUNTY!
YOU'RE NOT THE LAW IN THESE PARTS, AND I'M PERFORMING A CITIZENS' ARREST! HOW DO YA LIKE THEM APPLES, BOYS?
@#%@☆!
AND AT LAST --
THIS IS IT? THE WORLD-FAMOUS FALL FOLIAGE WE CAME TO SEE? ->PFAW!<-
NOW THAT THE PROPER AUTHORITIES HAVE STRIPPED THOSE GUYS OF ALL THEIR LEGAL POWER AND PUT 'EM BEHIND BARS...
SAY! WHAT GIVES WITH THE OVERGROWN GIZMO?
...I THINK IT'S TIME TO SET THINGS RIGHT HERE IN OGOWANWADDAYADOO COUNTY.
SPRAY!!
OH, MICKEY! AFTER ALL THAT'S HAPPENED, I THINK MAYBE THE TREES LOOK EVEN MORE BEAUTIFUL THAN BEFORE!
SHUCKS! I GUESS MAYBE THE "REAL WORLD CAN WAIT ANOTHER WEE BEFORE WE HAVE TO RETURN TO IT!
The End

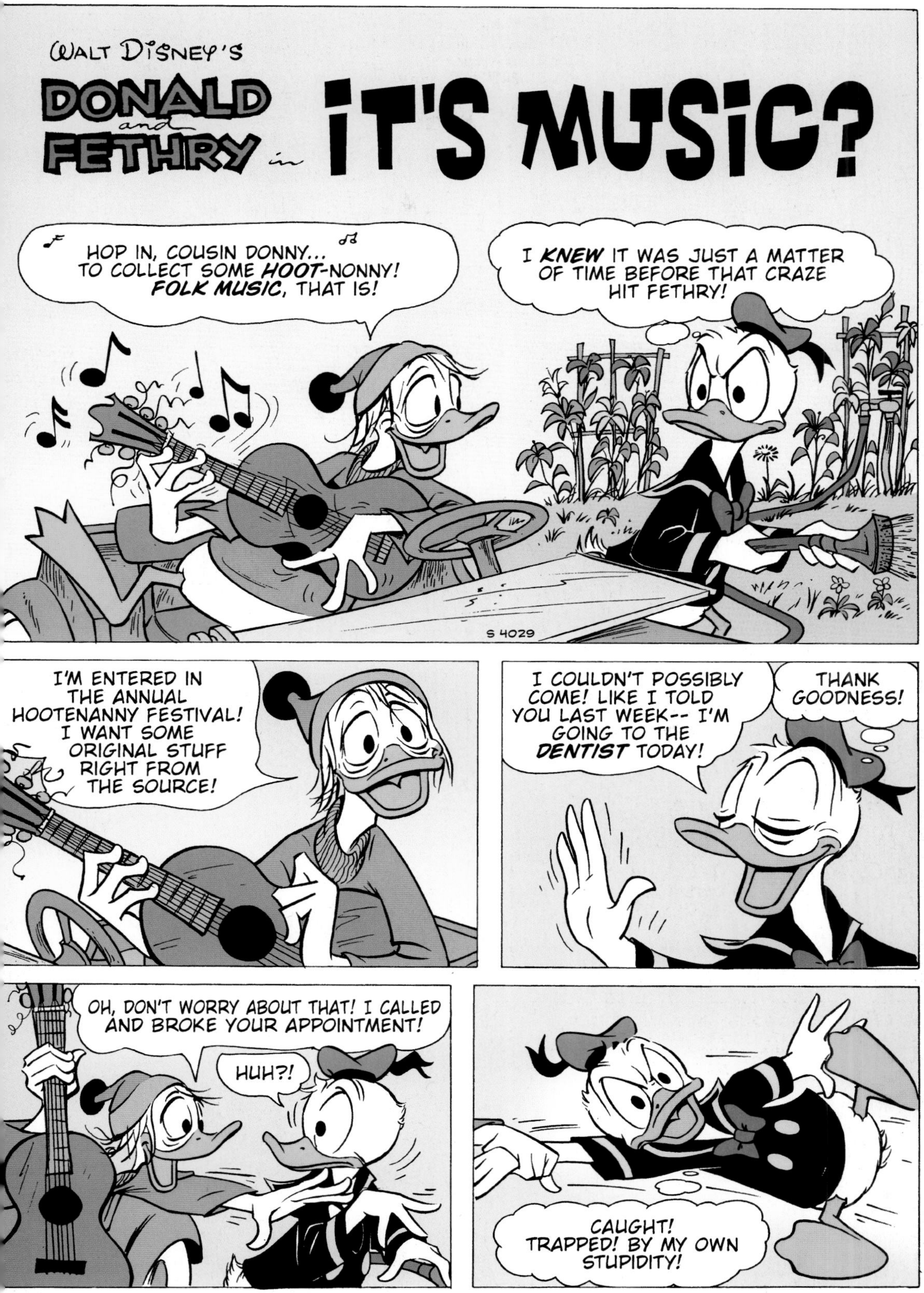

WALT DISNEY'S
DONALD and FETHRY in
IT'S MUSIC?
HOP IN, COUSIN DONNY... TO COLLECT SOME HOOT-NONNY! FOLK MUSIC, THAT IS!
I KNEW IT WAS JUST A MATTER OF TIME BEFORE THAT CRAZE HIT FETHRY!
S 4029
I'M ENTERED IN THE ANNUAL HOOTENANNY FESTIVAL! I WANT SOME ORIGINAL STUFF RIGHT FROM THE SOURCE!
I COULDN'T POSSIBLY COME! LIKE I TOLD YOU LAST WEEK-- I'M GOING TO THE DENTIST TODAY!
THANK GOODNESS!
OH, DON'T WORRY ABOUT THAT! I CALLED AND BROKE YOUR APPOINTMENT!
HUH?!
CAUGHT! TRAPPED! BY MY OWN STUPIDITY!

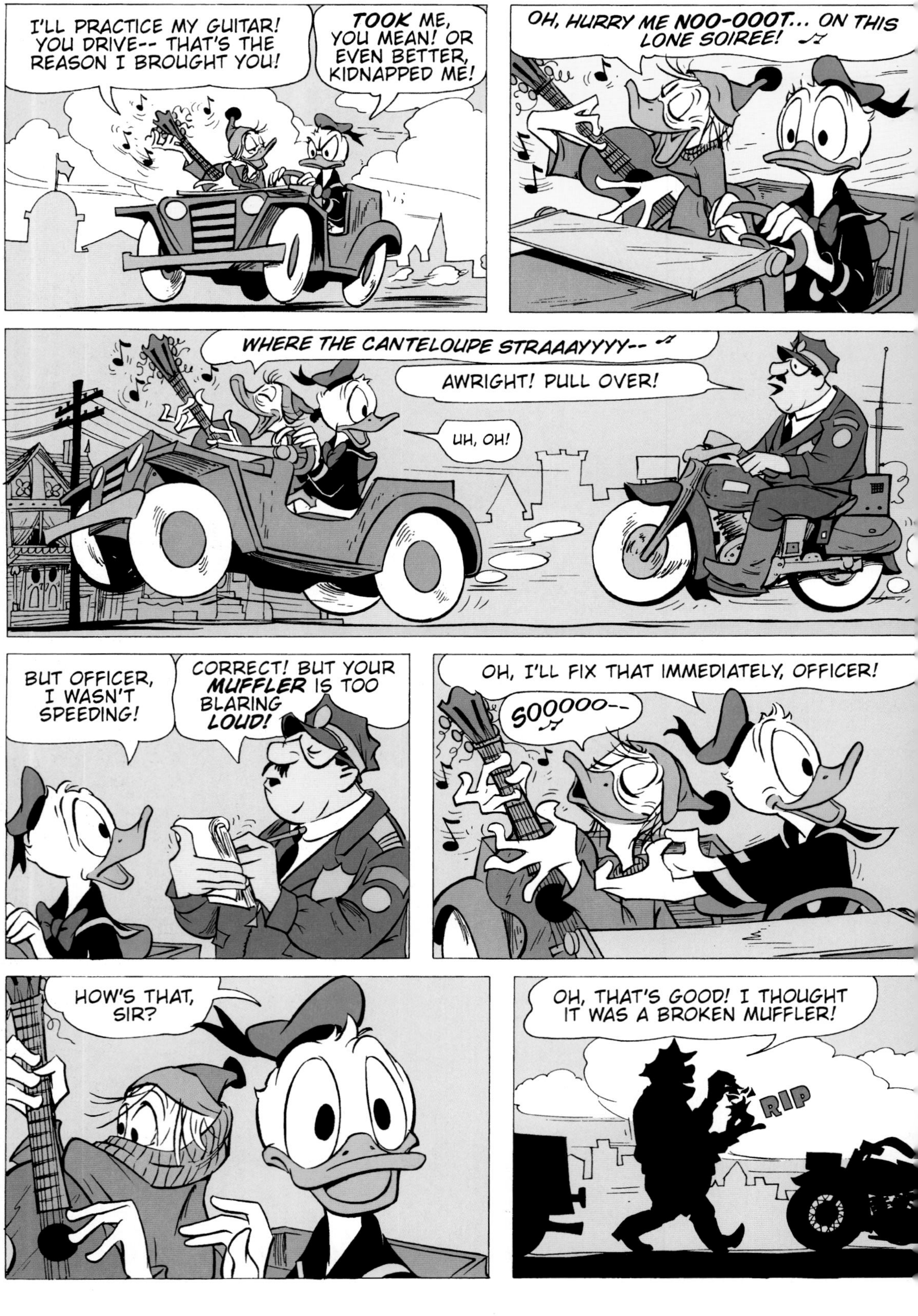
I'LL PRACTICE MY GUITAR! YOU DRIVE-- THAT'S THE REASON I BROUGHT YOU!
TOOK ME, YOU MEAN! OR EVEN BETTER, KIDNAPPED ME!
OH, HURRY ME NOO-OOOT... ON THIS LONE SOIREE!
WHERE THE CANTELOUPE STRAAAYYYY--
AWRIGHT! PULL OVER!
UH, OH!
BUT OFFICER, I WASN'T SPEEDING!
CORRECT! BUT YOUR MUFFLER IS TOO BLARING LOUD!
OH, I'LL FIX THAT IMMEDIATELY, OFFICER!
SOOOOO--
HOW'S THAT, SIR?
OH, THAT'S GOOD! I THOUGHT IT WAS A BROKEN MUFFLER!
RIP

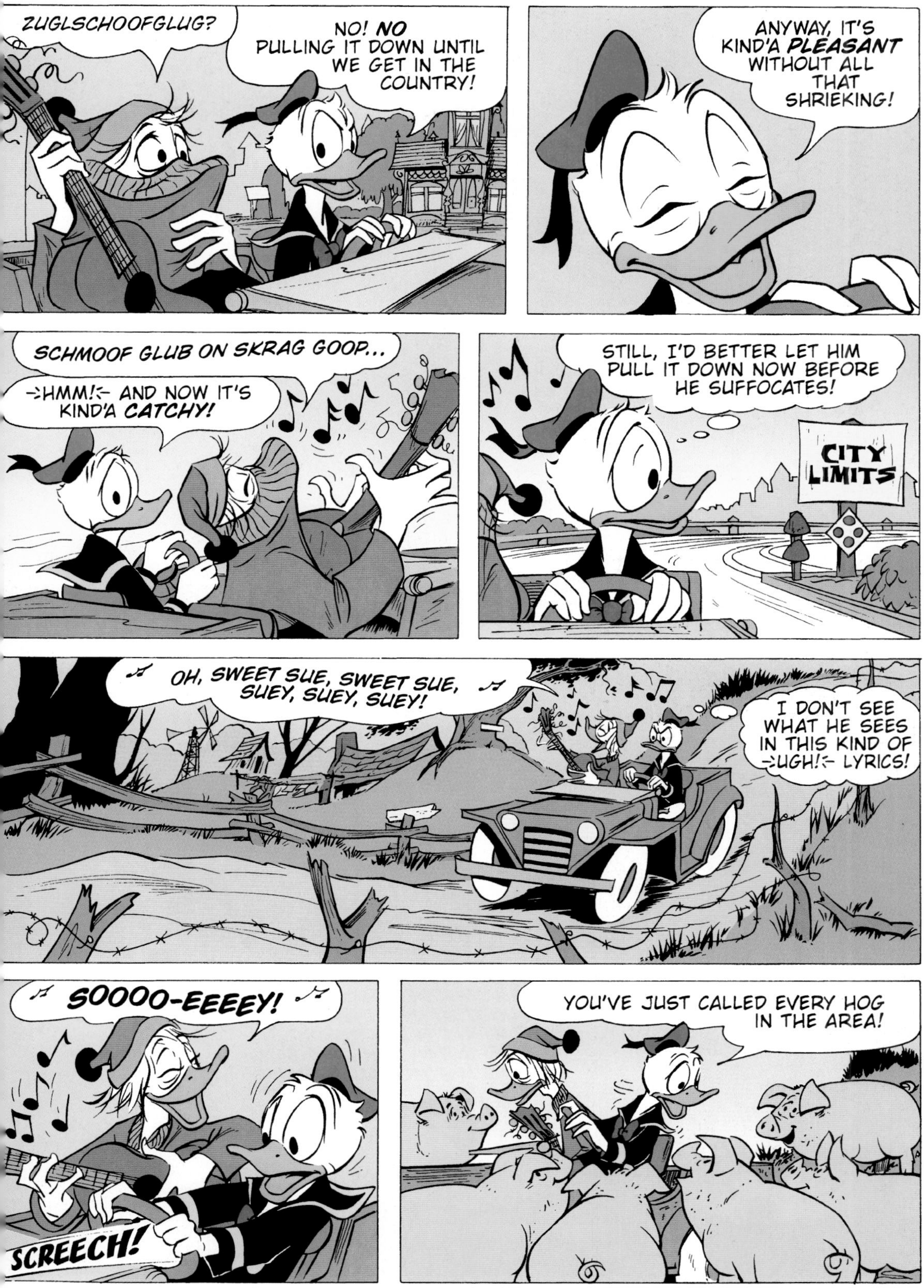
ZUGLSCHOOFGLUG?
NO! NO PULLING IT DOWN UNTIL WE GET IN THE COUNTRY!
ANYWAY, IT'S KIND'A PLEASANT WITHOUT ALL THAT SHRIEKING!
SCHMOOF GLUB ON SKRAG GOOP...
HMM! AND NOW IT'S KIND'A CATCHY!
STILL, I'D BETTER LET HIM PULL IT DOWN NOW BEFORE HE SUFFOCATES!
CITY LIMITS
OH, SWEET SUE, SWEET SUE, SUEY, SUEY, SUEY!
I DON'T SEE WHAT HE SEES IN THIS KIND OF UGH! LYRICS!
SOOOO-EEEEY!
SCREECH!
YOU'VE JUST CALLED EVERY HOG IN THE AREA!

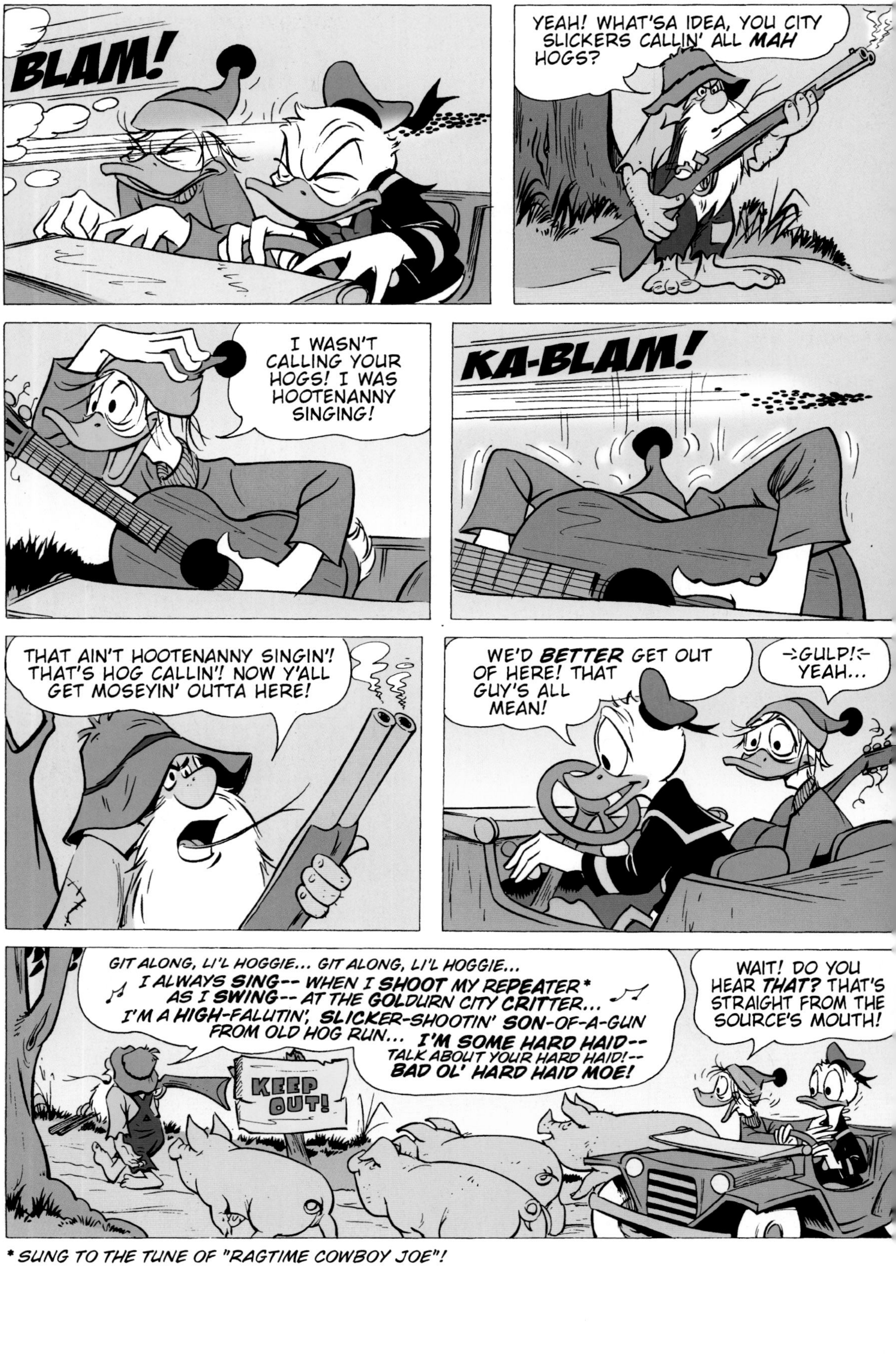
BLAM!
YEAH! WHAT'SA IDEA, YOU CITY SLICKERS CALLIN' ALL MAH HOGS?
I WASN'T CALLING YOUR HOGS! I WAS HOOTENANNY SINGING!
KA-BLAM!
THAT AIN'T HOOTENANNY SINGIN'! THAT'S HOG CALLIN'! NOW Y'ALL GET MOSEYIN' OUTTA HERE!
WE'D BETTER GET OUT OF HERE! THAT GUY'S ALL MEAN!
GULP! YEAH...
GIT ALONG, LI'L HOGGIE... GIT ALONG, LI'L HOGGIE... I ALWAYS SING-- WHEN I SHOOT MY REPEATER* AS I SWING-- AT THE GOLDURN CITY CRITTER... I'M A HIGH-FALUTIN', SLICKER-SHOOTIN' SON-OF-A-GUN FROM OLD HOG RUN... I'M SOME HARD HAID-- TALK ABOUT YOUR HARD HAID!-- BAD OL' HARD HAID MOE!
KEEP OUT!
WAIT! DO YOU HEAR THAT? THAT'S STRAIGHT FROM THE SOURCE'S MOUTH!

* SUNG TO THE TUNE OF "RAGTIME COWBOY JOE"!

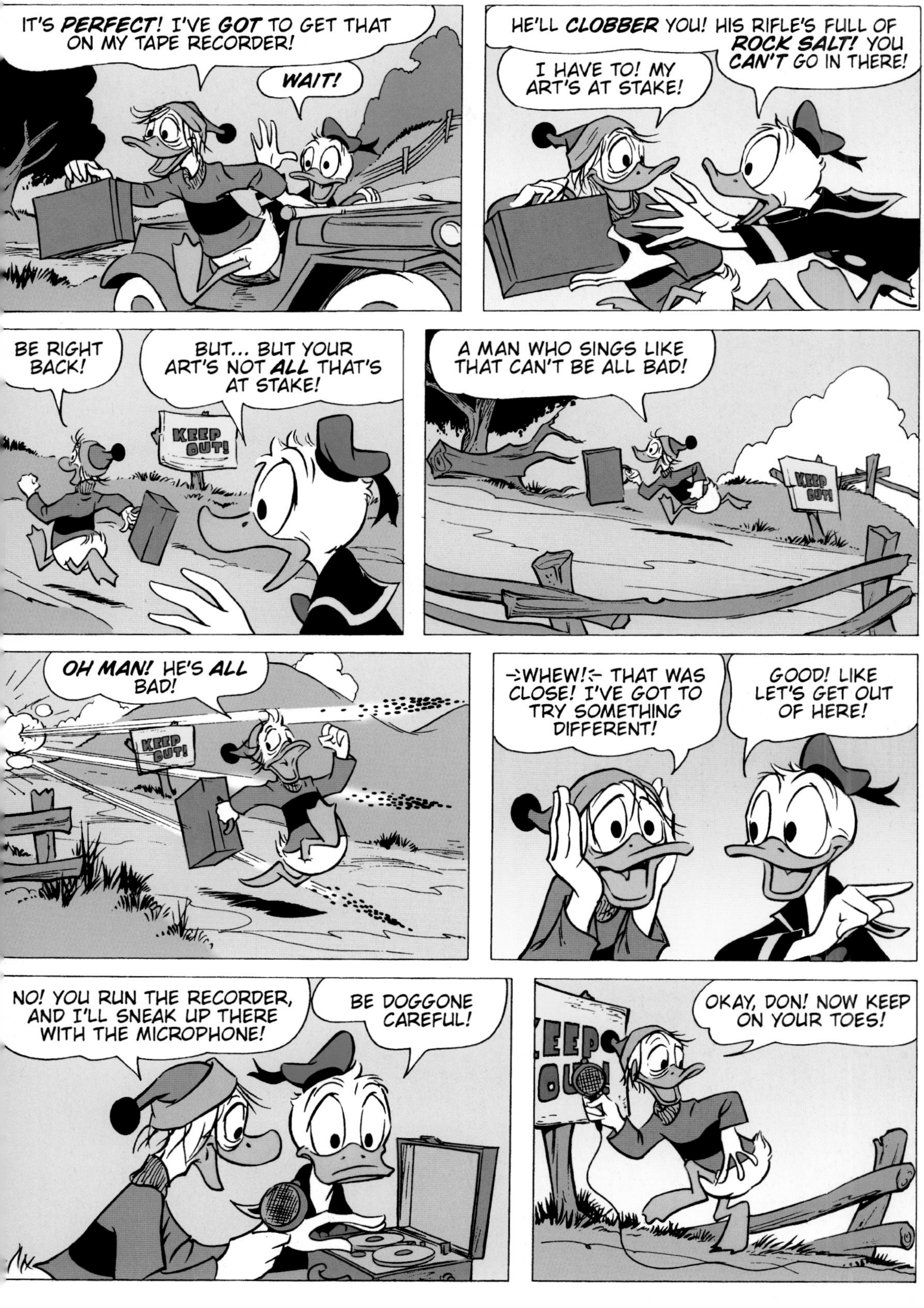
IT'S PERFECT! I'VE GOT TO GET THAT ON MY TAPE RECORDER!
WAIT!
HE'LL CLOBBER YOU! HIS RIFLE'S FULL OF ROCK SALT! YOU CAN'T GO IN THERE!
I HAVE TO! MY ART'S AT STAKE!
BE RIGHT BACK!
BUT... BUT YOUR ART'S NOT ALL THAT'S AT STAKE!
KEEP OUT!
A MAN WHO SINGS LIKE THAT CAN'T BE ALL BAD!
KEEP OUT!
OH MAN! HE'S ALL BAD!
KEEP OUT!
WHEW! THAT WAS CLOSE! I'VE GOT TO TRY SOMETHING DIFFERENT!
GOOD! LIKE LET'S GET OUT OF HERE!
NO! YOU RUN THE RECORDER, AND I'LL SNEAK UP THERE WITH THE MICROPHONE!
BE DOGGONE CAREFUL!
OKAY, DON! NOW KEEP ON YOUR TOES!

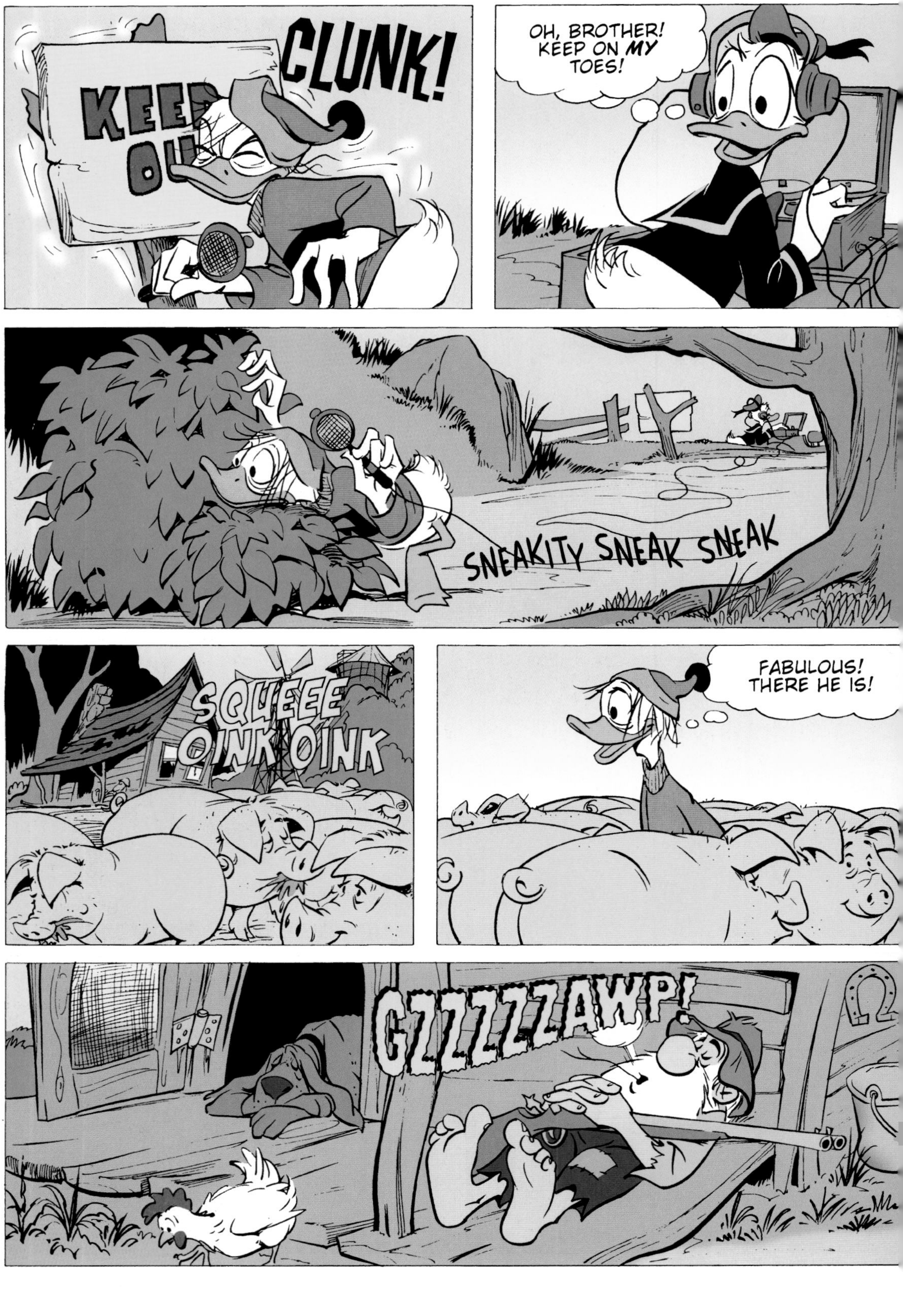
KEEP OUT
CLUNK!
OH, BROTHER! KEEP ON MY TOES!
SNEAKITY SNEAK SNEAK
SQUEEE OINK OINK
FABULOUS! THERE HE IS!
GZZZZZAWP!

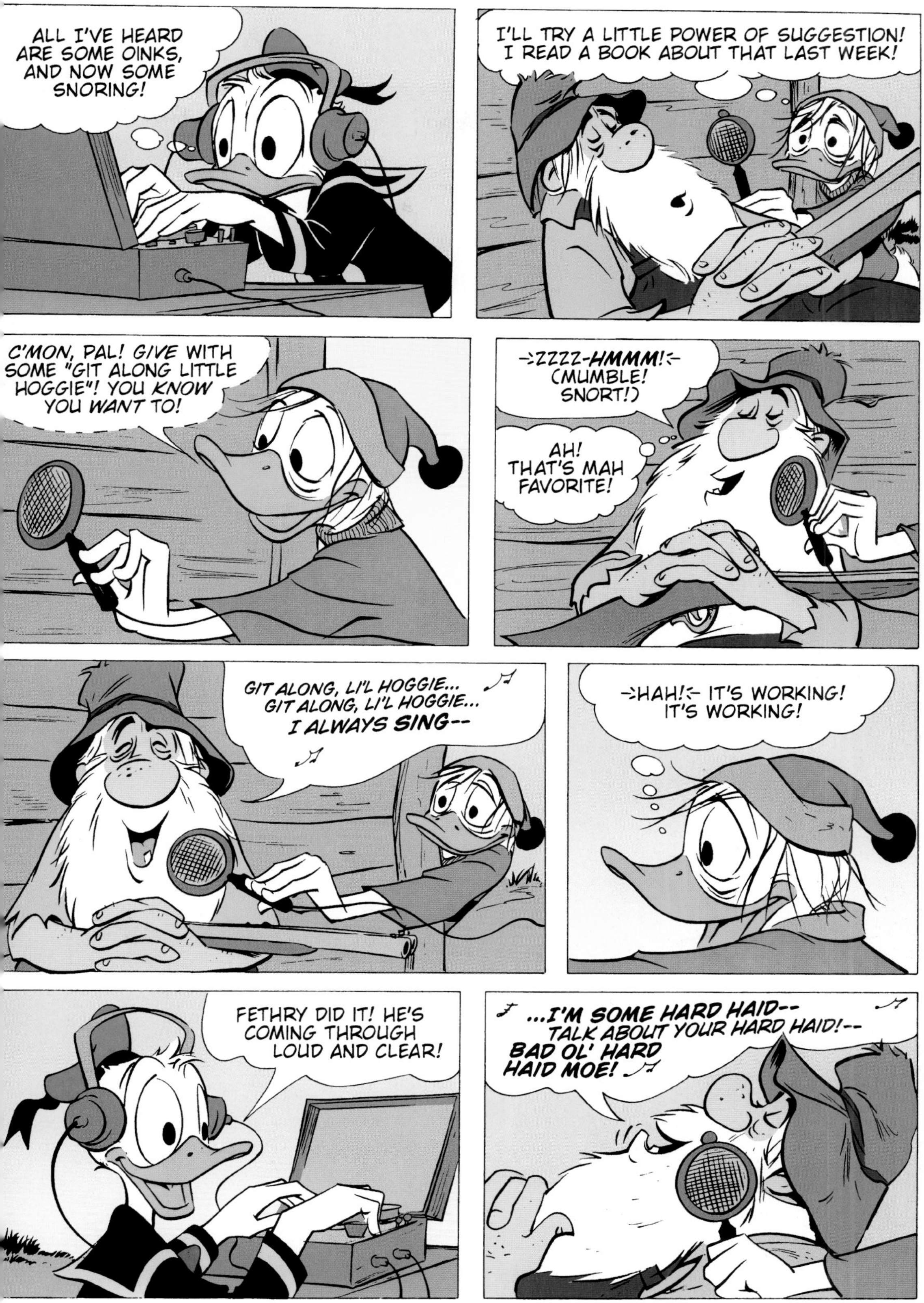
ALL I'VE HEARD ARE SOME OINKS, AND NOW SOME SNORING!
I'LL TRY A LITTLE POWER OF SUGGESTION! I READ A BOOK ABOUT THAT LAST WEEK!
C'MON, PAL! GIVE WITH SOME "GIT ALONG LITTLE HOGGIE"! YOU KNOW YOU WANT TO!
ZZZZ-HMMM! (MUMBLE! SNORT!)
AH! THAT'S MAH FAVORITE!
GIT ALONG, LI'L HOGGIE... GIT ALONG, LI'L HOGGIE... I ALWAYS SING--
HAH! IT'S WORKING! IT'S WORKING!
FETHRY DID IT! HE'S COMING THROUGH LOUD AND CLEAR!
...I'M SOME HARD HAID-- TALK ABOUT YOUR HARD HAID!-- BAD OL' HARD HAID MOE!

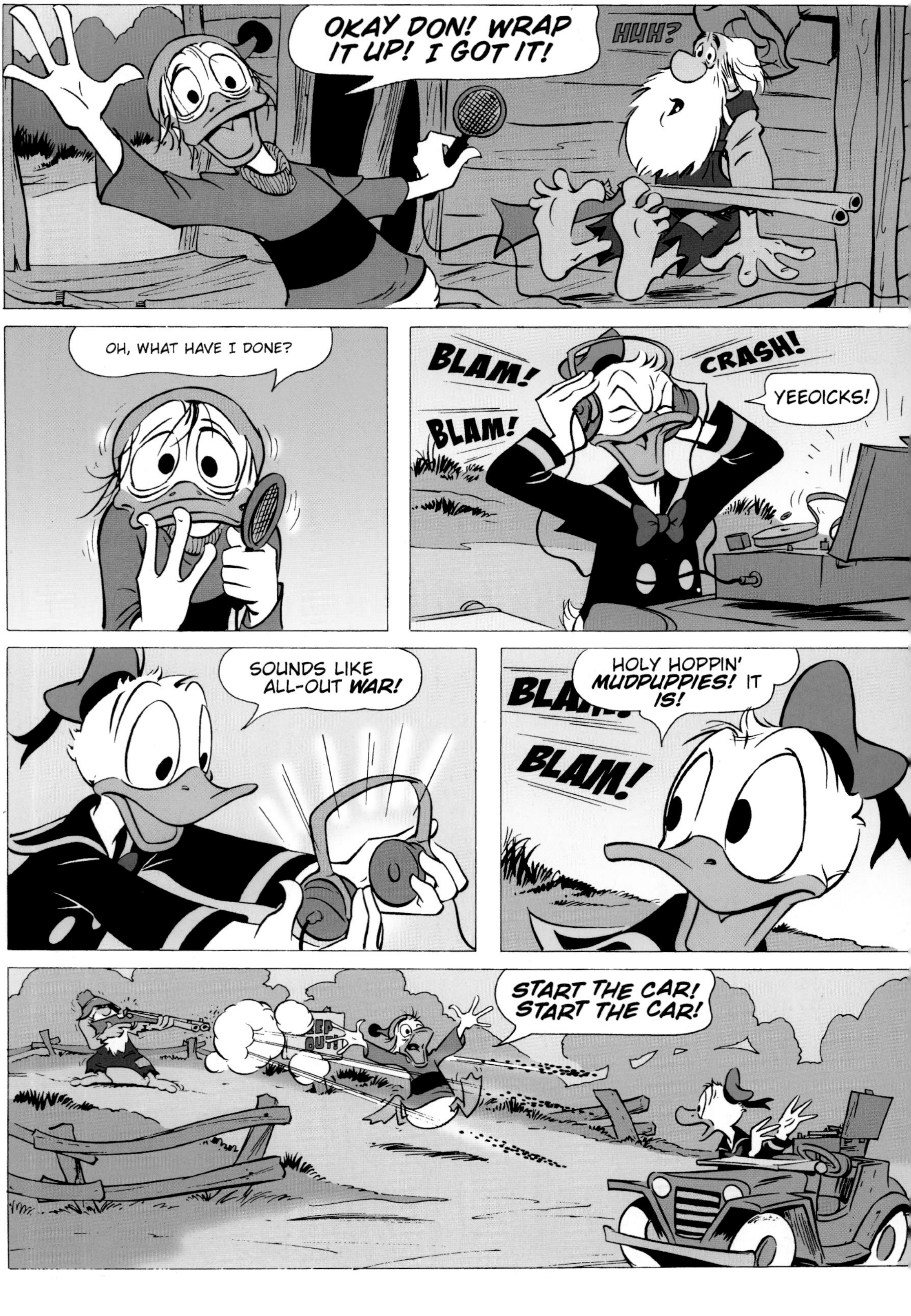
OKAY DON! WRAP IT UP! I GOT IT!
HUH?
OH, WHAT HAVE I DONE?
BLAM!
CRASH!
YEEOICKS!
BLAM!
SOUNDS LIKE ALL-OUT WAR!
HOLY HOPPIN' MUDPUPPIES! IT IS!
BLAM!
START THE CAR! START THE CAR!

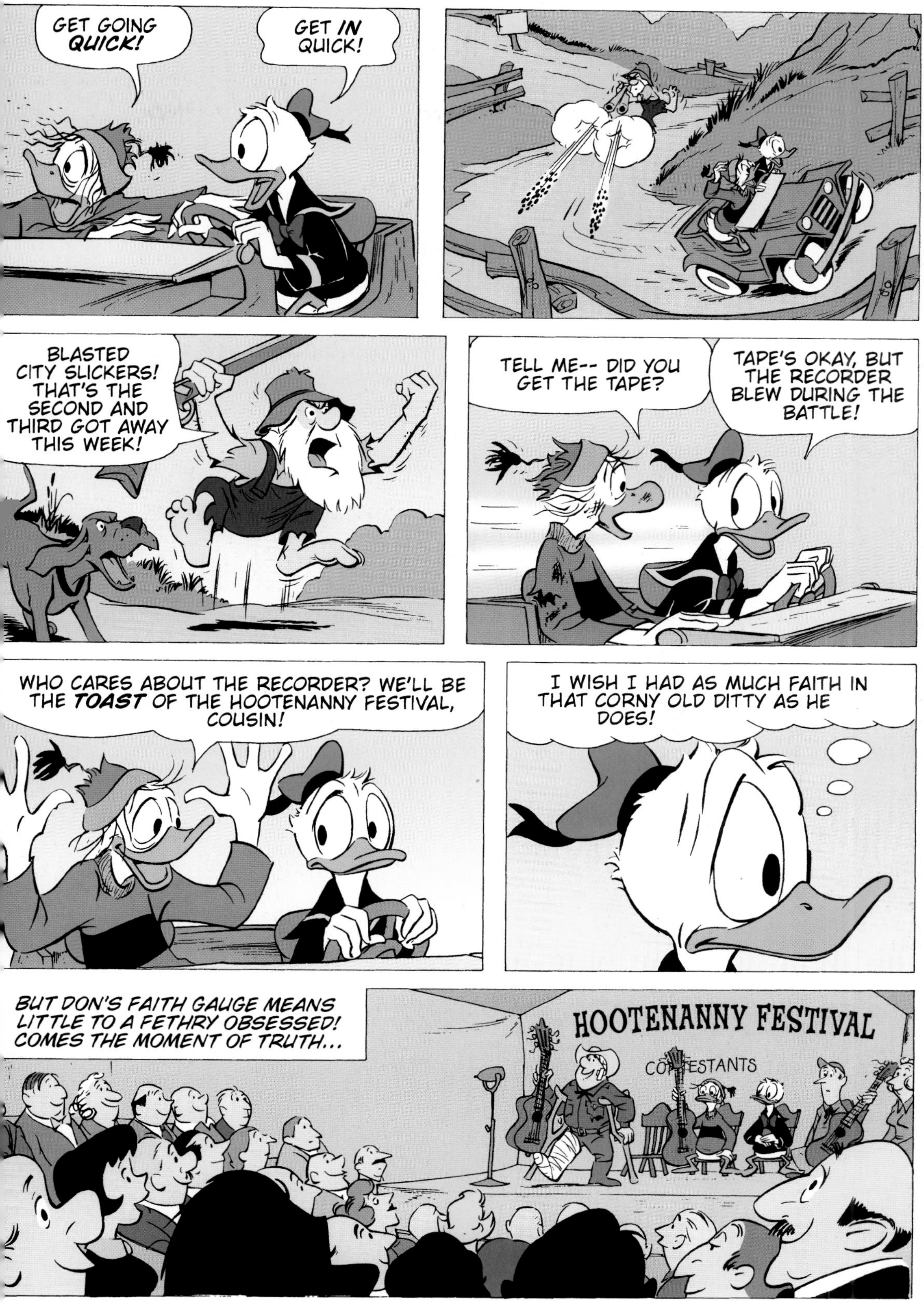
GET GOING QUICK!
GET IN QUICK!
BLASTED CITY SLICKERS! THAT'S THE SECOND AND THIRD GOT AWAY THIS WEEK!
TELL ME-- DID YOU GET THE TAPE?
TAPE'S OKAY, BUT THE RECORDER BLEW DURING THE BATTLE!
WHO CARES ABOUT THE RECORDER? WE'LL BE THE TOAST OF THE HOOTENANNY FESTIVAL, COUSIN!
I WISH I HAD AS MUCH FAITH IN THAT CORNY OLD DITTY AS HE DOES!
BUT DON'S FAITH GAUGE MEANS LITTLE TO A FETHRY OBSESSED! COMES THE MOMENT OF TRUTH...
HOOTENANNY FESTIVAL
CONTESTANTS

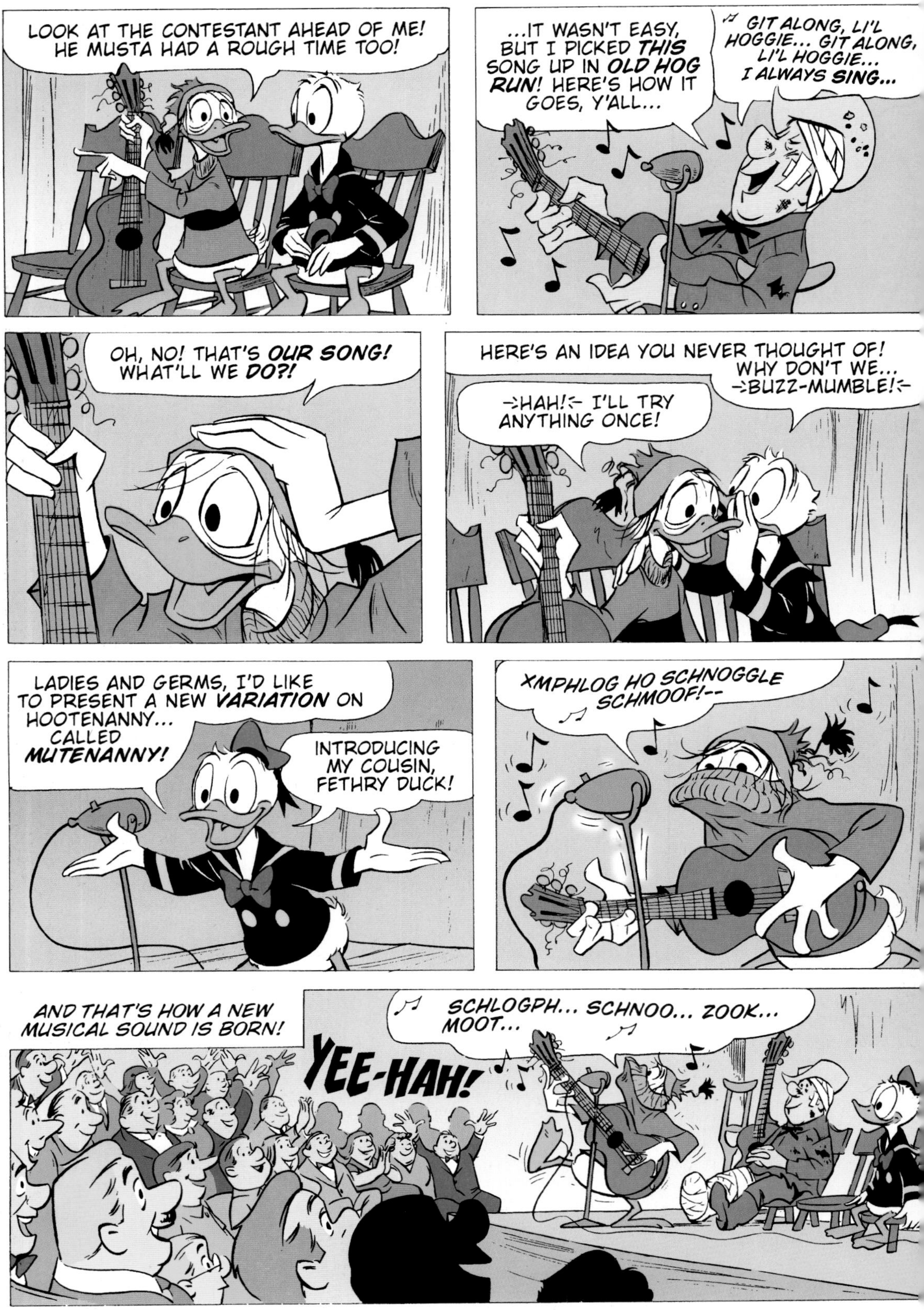
LOOK AT THE CONTESTANT AHEAD OF ME! HE MUSTA HAD A ROUGH TIME TOO!
...IT WASN'T EASY, BUT I PICKED THIS SONG UP IN OLD HOG RUN! HERE'S HOW IT GOES, Y'ALL...
GIT ALONG, LI'L HOGGIE... GIT ALONG, LI'L HOGGIE... I ALWAYS SING...
OH, NO! THAT'S OUR SONG! WHAT'LL WE DO?!
HERE'S AN IDEA YOU NEVER THOUGHT OF! WHY DON'T WE... -BUZZ-MUMBLE!-
-HAH!- I'LL TRY ANYTHING ONCE!
LADIES AND GERMS, I'D LIKE TO PRESENT A NEW VARIATION ON HOOTENANNY... CALLED MUTENANNY!
INTRODUCING MY COUSIN, FETHRY DUCK!
XMPHLOG HO SCHNOGGLE SCHMOOF!--
AND THAT'S HOW A NEW MUSICAL SOUND IS BORN!
SCHLOGPH... SCHNOO... ZOOK... MOOT...
YEE-HAH!

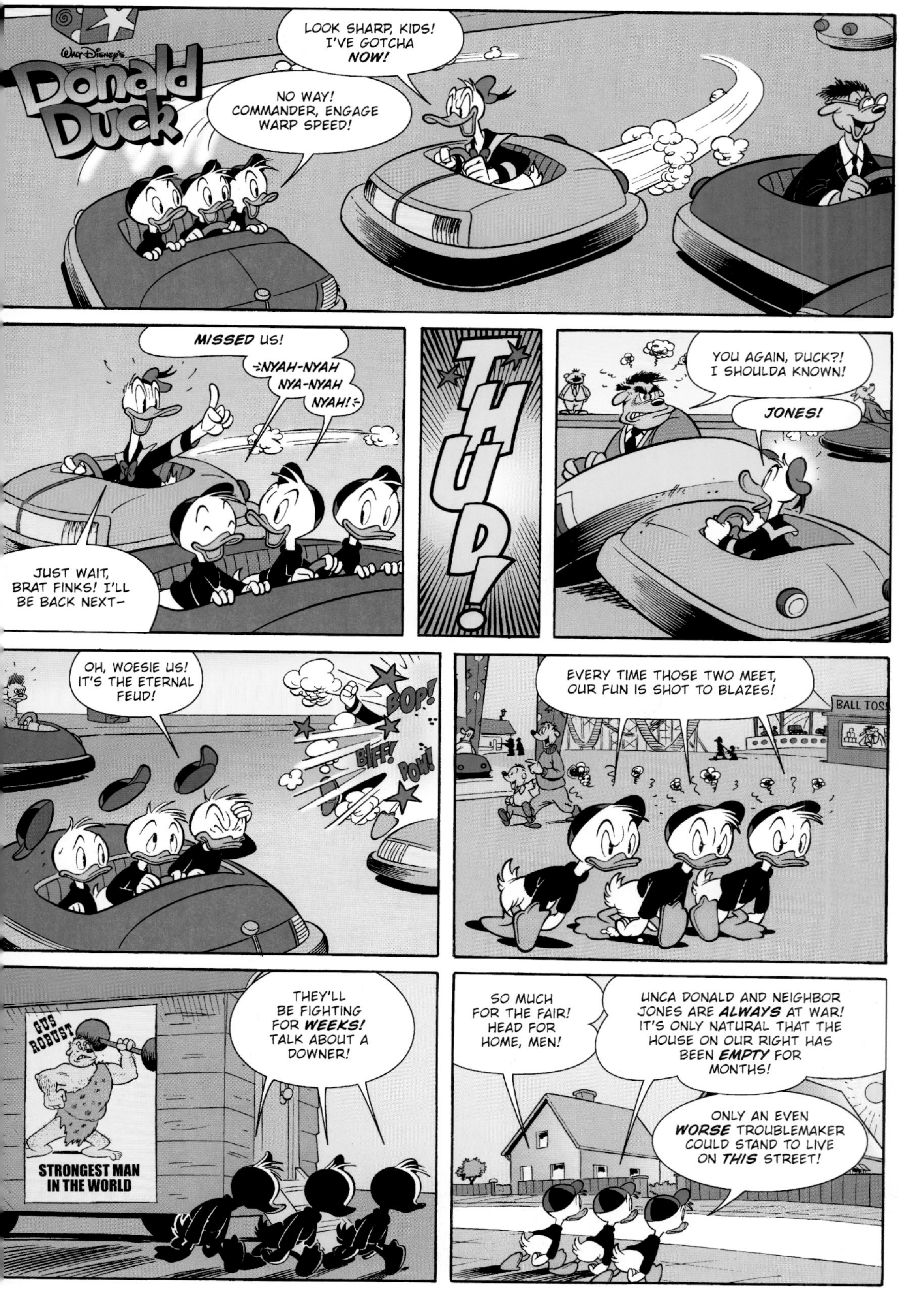
Walt Disney's
Donald Duck
LOOK SHARP, KIDS! I'VE GOTCHA NOW!
NO WAY! COMMANDER, ENGAGE WARP SPEED!
MISSED US!
NYAH-NYAH NYA-NYAH NYAH!
JUST WAIT, BRAT FINKS! I'LL BE BACK NEXT—
THUD!
YOU AGAIN, DUCK?! I SHOULDA KNOWN!
JONES!
OH, WOESIE US! IT'S THE ETERNAL FEUD!
BOP!
BIFF!
POW!
EVERY TIME THOSE TWO MEET, OUR FUN IS SHOT TO BLAZES!
BALL TOSS
GUS ROBUST
STRONGEST MAN IN THE WORLD
THEY'LL BE FIGHTING FOR WEEKS! TALK ABOUT A DOWNER!
SO MUCH FOR THE FAIR! HEAD FOR HOME, MEN!
UNCA DONALD AND NEIGHBOR JONES ARE ALWAYS AT WAR! IT'S ONLY NATURAL THAT THE HOUSE ON OUR RIGHT HAS BEEN EMPTY FOR MONTHS!
ONLY AN EVEN WORSE TROUBLEMAKER COULD STAND TO LIVE ON THIS STREET!

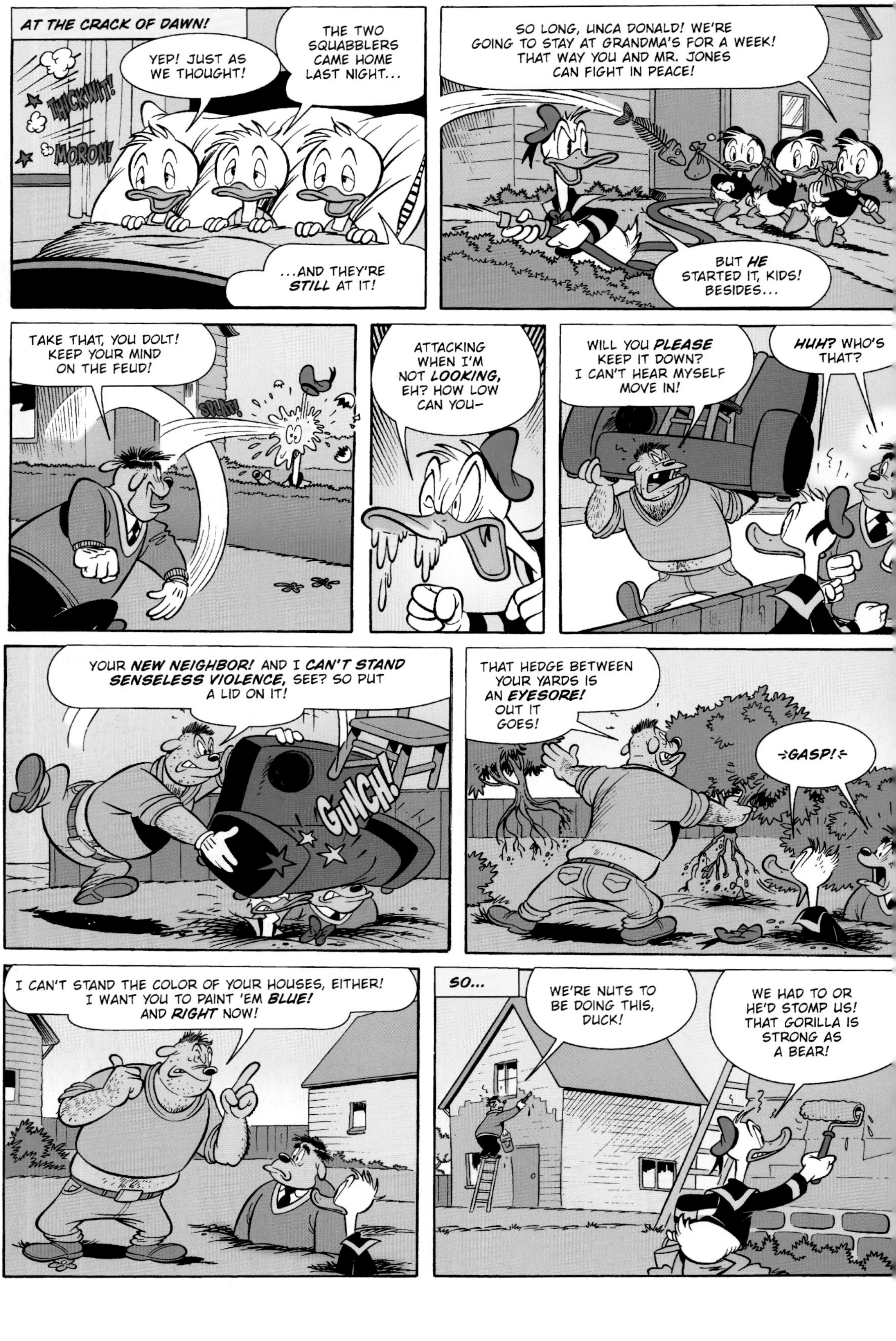
AT THE CRACK OF DAWN!
THICKWIT!
MORON!
YEP! JUST AS WE THOUGHT!
THE TWO SQUABBLERS CAME HOME LAST NIGHT...
...AND THEY'RE STILL AT IT!
SO LONG, UNCA DONALD! WE'RE GOING TO STAY AT GRANDMA'S FOR A WEEK! THAT WAY YOU AND MR. JONES CAN FIGHT IN PEACE!
BUT HE STARTED IT, KIDS! BESIDES...
TAKE THAT, YOU DOLT! KEEP YOUR MIND ON THE FEUD!
SPLAT!
ATTACKING WHEN I'M NOT LOOKING, EH? HOW LOW CAN YOU-
WILL YOU PLEASE KEEP IT DOWN? I CAN'T HEAR MYSELF MOVE IN!
HUH? WHO'S THAT?
YOUR NEW NEIGHBOR! AND I CAN'T STAND SENSELESS VIOLENCE, SEE? SO PUT A LID ON IT!
GUNCH!
THAT HEDGE BETWEEN YOUR YARDS IS AN EYESORE! OUT IT GOES!
GASP!
I CAN'T STAND THE COLOR OF YOUR HOUSES, EITHER! I WANT YOU TO PAINT 'EM BLUE! AND RIGHT NOW!
SO...
WE'RE NUTS TO BE DOING THIS, DUCK!
WE HAD TO OR HE'D STOMP US! THAT GORILLA IS STRONG AS A BEAR!

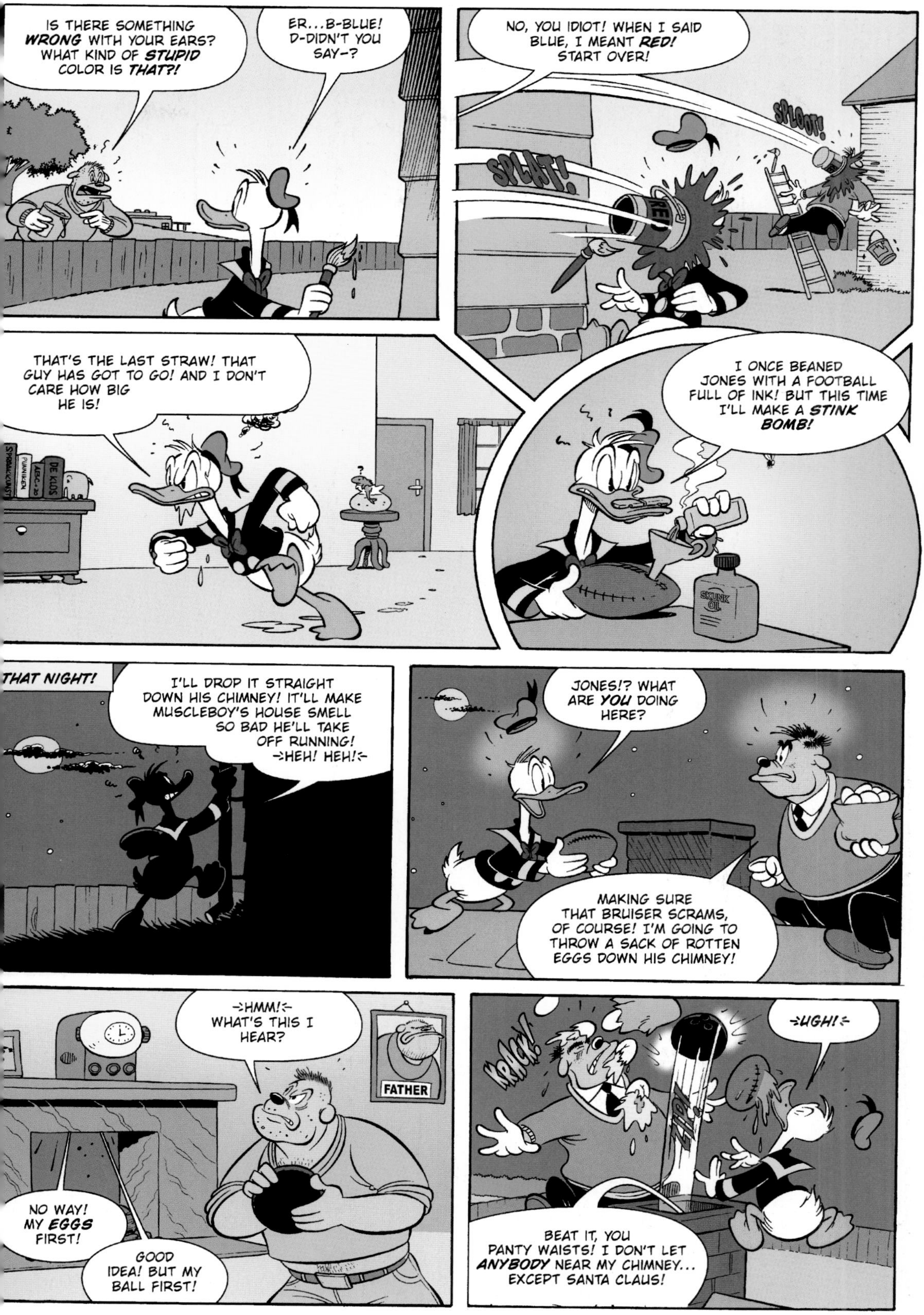
IS THERE SOMETHING WRONG WITH YOUR EARS? WHAT KIND OF STUPID COLOR IS THAT?!
ER...B-BLUE! D-DIDN'T YOU SAY–?
NO, YOU IDIOT! WHEN I SAID BLUE, I MEANT RED! START OVER!
SPLAT!
SPLOOT!
RED
THAT'S THE LAST STRAW! THAT GUY HAS GOT TO GO! AND I DON'T CARE HOW BIG HE IS!
I ONCE BEANED JONES WITH A FOOTBALL FULL OF INK! BUT THIS TIME I'LL MAKE A STINK BOMB!
SKUNK OIL
THAT NIGHT!
I'LL DROP IT STRAIGHT DOWN HIS CHIMNEY! IT'LL MAKE MUSCLEBOY'S HOUSE SMELL SO BAD HE'LL TAKE OFF RUNNING! –HEH! HEH!–
JONES!? WHAT ARE YOU DOING HERE?
MAKING SURE THAT BRUISER SCRAMS, OF COURSE! I'M GOING TO THROW A SACK OF ROTTEN EGGS DOWN HIS CHIMNEY!
–HMM!– WHAT'S THIS I HEAR?
FATHER
NO WAY! MY EGGS FIRST!
GOOD IDEA! BUT MY BALL FIRST!
KRACK!
–UGH!–
BEAT IT, YOU PANTY WAISTS! I DON'T LET ANYBODY NEAR MY CHIMNEY... EXCEPT SANTA CLAUS!

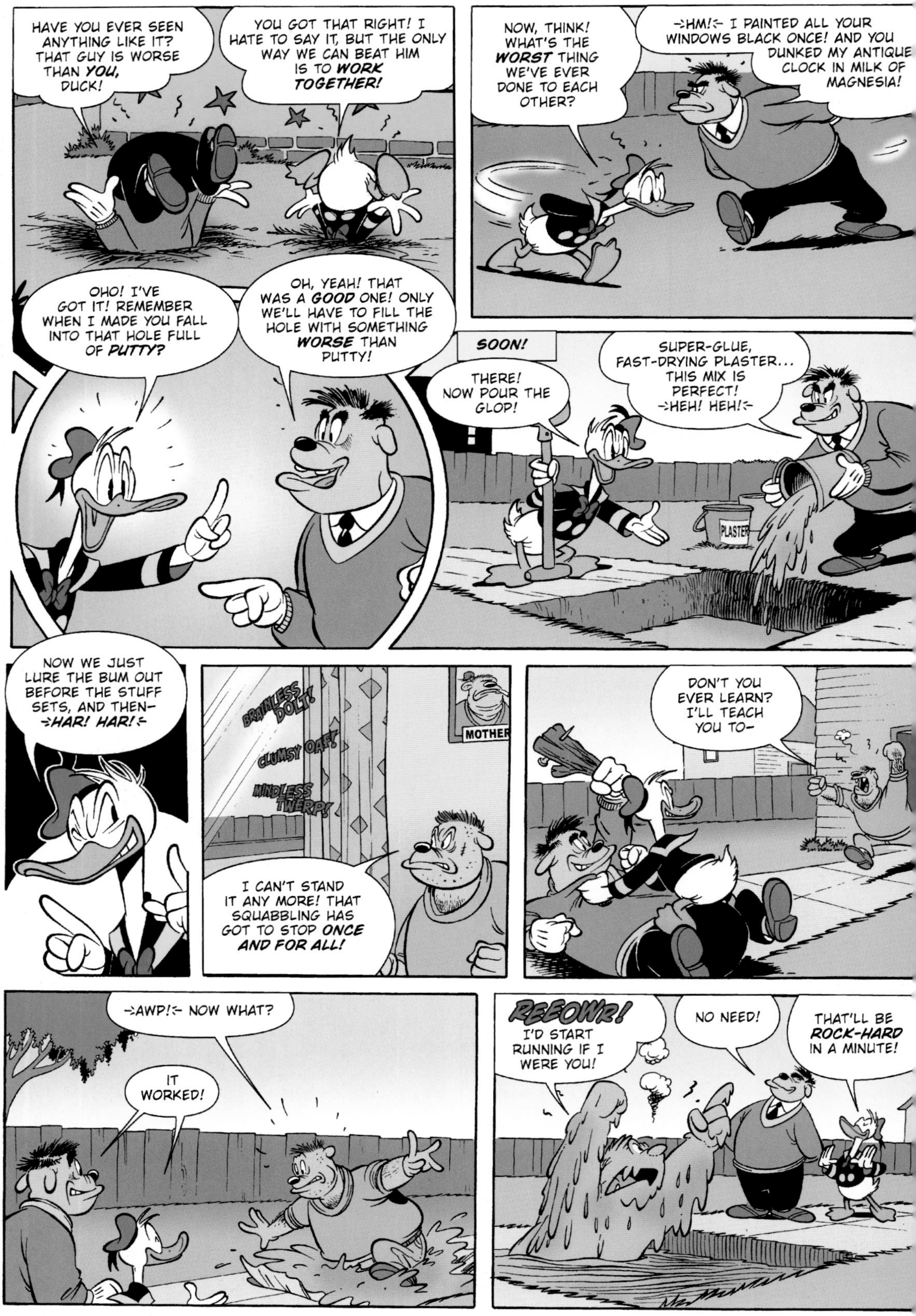

HAVE YOU EVER SEEN ANYTHING LIKE IT? THAT GUY IS WORSE THAN YOU, DUCK!
YOU GOT THAT RIGHT! I HATE TO SAY IT, BUT THE ONLY WAY WE CAN BEAT HIM IS TO WORK TOGETHER!
NOW, THINK! WHAT'S THE WORST THING WE'VE EVER DONE TO EACH OTHER?
-HM!- I PAINTED ALL YOUR WINDOWS BLACK ONCE! AND YOU DUNKED MY ANTIQUE CLOCK IN MILK OF MAGNESIA!
OHO! I'VE GOT IT! REMEMBER WHEN I MADE YOU FALL INTO THAT HOLE FULL OF PUTTY?
OH, YEAH! THAT WAS A GOOD ONE! ONLY WE'LL HAVE TO FILL THE HOLE WITH SOMETHING WORSE THAN PUTTY!
SOON!
THERE! NOW POUR THE GLOP!
SUPER-GLUE, FAST-DRYING PLASTER... THIS MIX IS PERFECT! -HEH! HEH!-
PLASTER
NOW WE JUST LURE THE BUM OUT BEFORE THE STUFF SETS, AND THEN- -HAR! HAR!-
BRAINLESS DOLT!
CLUMSY OAF!
MINDLESS TWERP!
MOTHER
I CAN'T STAND IT ANY MORE! THAT SQUABBLING HAS GOT TO STOP ONCE AND FOR ALL!
DON'T YOU EVER LEARN? I'LL TEACH YOU TO-
-AWP!- NOW WHAT?
IT WORKED!
REEOWR!
I'D START RUNNING IF I WERE YOU!
NO NEED!
THAT'LL BE ROCK-HARD IN A MINUTE!

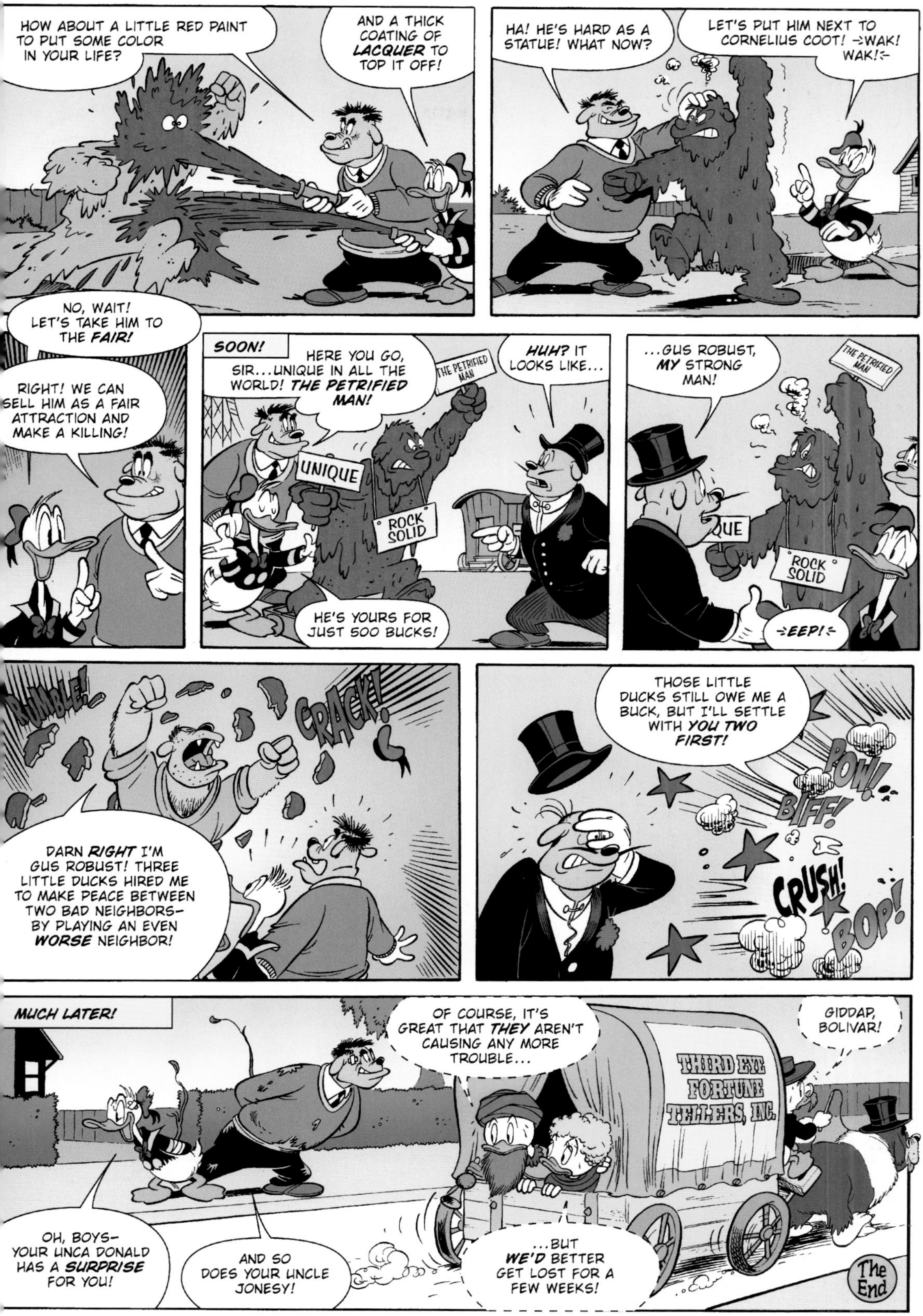
HOW ABOUT A LITTLE RED PAINT TO PUT SOME COLOR IN YOUR LIFE?
AND A THICK COATING OF LACQUER TO TOP IT OFF!
HA! HE'S HARD AS A STATUE! WHAT NOW?
LET'S PUT HIM NEXT TO CORNELIUS COOT! WAK! WAK!
NO, WAIT! LET'S TAKE HIM TO THE FAIR!
RIGHT! WE CAN SELL HIM AS A FAIR ATTRACTION AND MAKE A KILLING!
SOON!
HERE YOU GO, SIR... UNIQUE IN ALL THE WORLD! THE PETRIFIED MAN!
THE PETRIFIED MAN
UNIQUE
ROCK SOLID
HE'S YOURS FOR JUST 500 BUCKS!
HUH? IT LOOKS LIKE...
...GUS ROBUST, MY STRONG MAN!
THE PETRIFIED MAN
QUE
ROCK SOLID
EEP!
RUMBLE!
CRACK!
DARN RIGHT I'M GUS ROBUST! THREE LITTLE DUCKS HIRED ME TO MAKE PEACE BETWEEN TWO BAD NEIGHBORS– BY PLAYING AN EVEN WORSE NEIGHBOR!
THOSE LITTLE DUCKS STILL OWE ME A BUCK, BUT I'LL SETTLE WITH YOU TWO FIRST!
POW!
BIFF!
CRUSH!
BOP!
MUCH LATER!
OF COURSE, IT'S GREAT THAT THEY AREN'T CAUSING ANY MORE TROUBLE...
GIDDAP, BOLIVAR!
THIRD EYE FORTUNE TELLERS, INC.
OH, BOYS– YOUR UNCA DONALD HAS A SURPRISE FOR YOU!
AND SO DOES YOUR UNCLE JONESY!
...BUT WE'D BETTER GET LOST FOR A FEW WEEKS!
The End

© 2005 Disney
Enterprises Inc.

Delivered right to your door!

We know how much you enjoy visiting your local comic shop, but wouldn't it be nice to have your favorite Disney comics delivered to you? Subscribe today and we'll send the latest issues of your favorite comics directly to your doorstep. And if you would still prefer to browse through the latest in comic art but aren't sure where to go, check out the Comic Shop Locator Service at www.diamondcomics.com/csls or call 1-888-COMIC-BOOK.

Walt Disney's GOOFY in TWO LEFT FEET

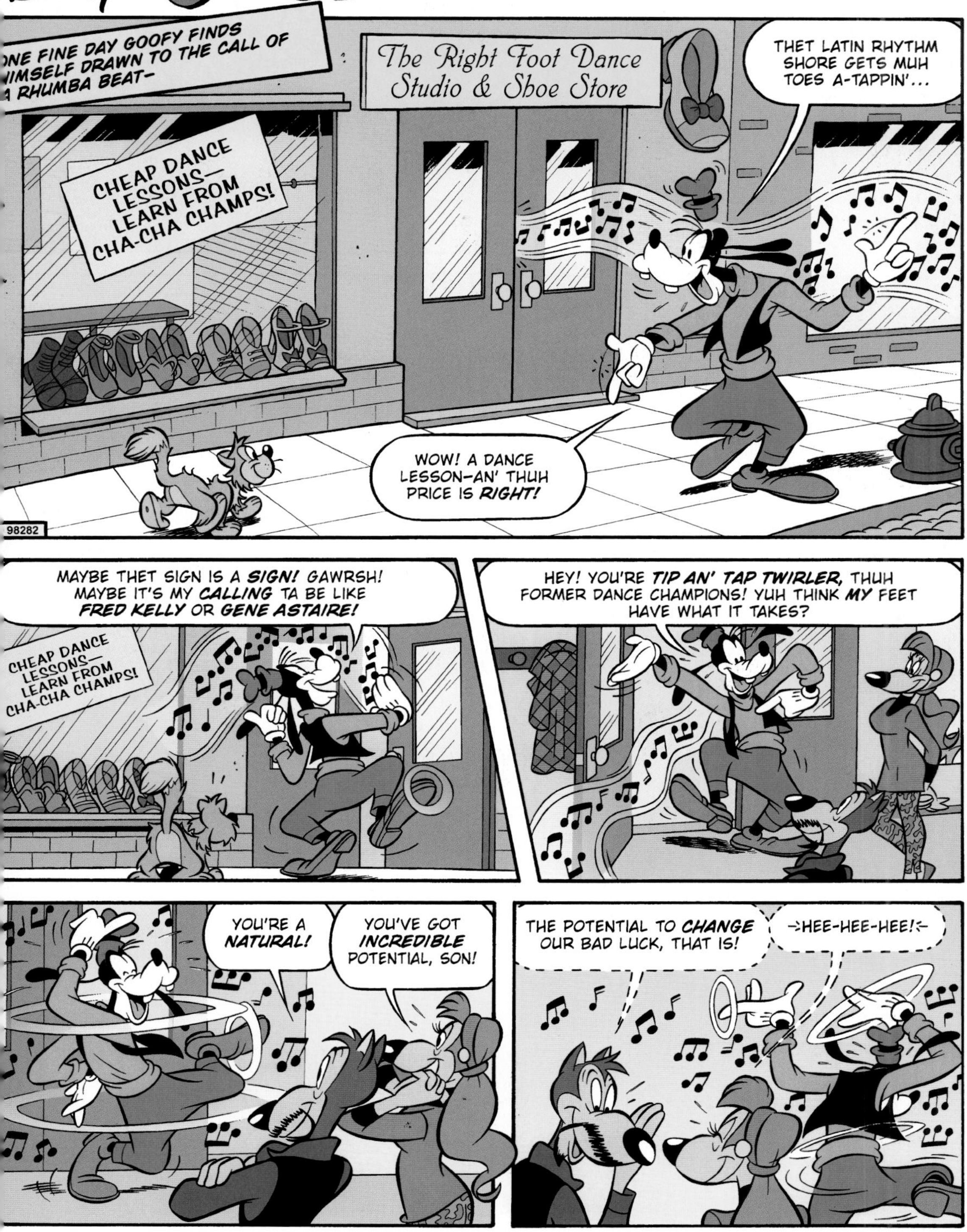

ONE FINE DAY GOOFY FINDS HIMSELF DRAWN TO THE CALL OF A RHUMBA BEAT–
The Right Foot Dance Studio & Shoe Store
CHEAP DANCE LESSONS— LEARN FROM CHA-CHA CHAMPS!
THET LATIN RHYTHM SHORE GETS MUH TOES A-TAPPIN'...
WOW! A DANCE LESSON–AN' THUH PRICE IS RIGHT!
98282
MAYBE THET SIGN IS A SIGN! GAWRSH! MAYBE IT'S MY CALLING TA BE LIKE FRED KELLY OR GENE ASTAIRE!
CHEAP DANCE LESSONS— LEARN FROM CHA-CHA CHAMPS!
HEY! YOU'RE TIP AN' TAP TWIRLER, THUH FORMER DANCE CHAMPIONS! YUH THINK MY FEET HAVE WHAT IT TAKES?
YOU'RE A NATURAL!
YOU'VE GOT INCREDIBLE POTENTIAL, SON!
THE POTENTIAL TO CHANGE OUR BAD LUCK, THAT IS!
HEE-HEE-HEE!

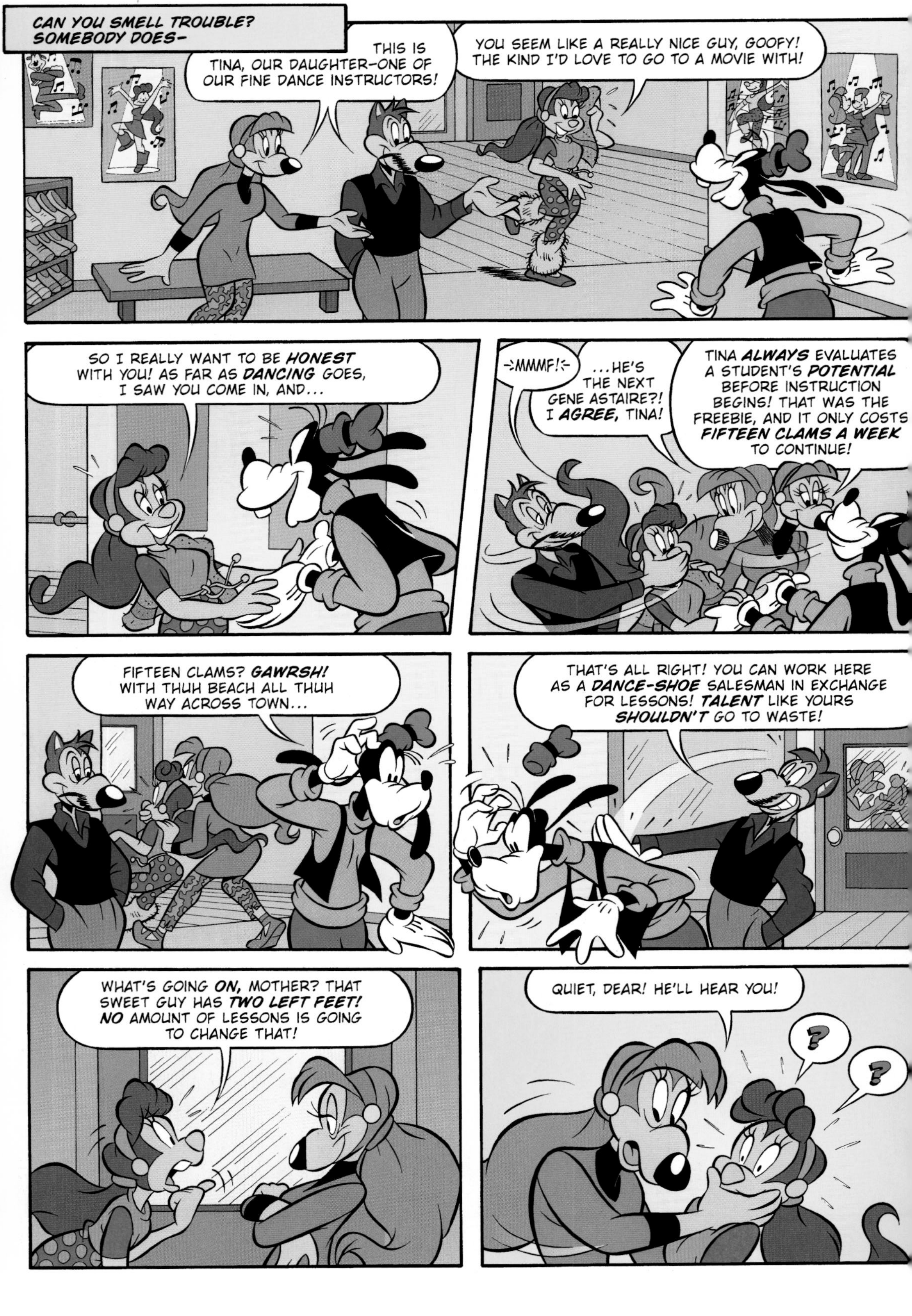
CAN YOU SMELL TROUBLE? SOMEBODY DOES–
THIS IS TINA, OUR DAUGHTER–ONE OF OUR FINE DANCE INSTRUCTORS!
YOU SEEM LIKE A REALLY NICE GUY, GOOFY! THE KIND I'D LOVE TO GO TO A MOVIE WITH!
SO I REALLY WANT TO BE HONEST WITH YOU! AS FAR AS DANCING GOES, I SAW YOU COME IN, AND...
MMMF!
...HE'S THE NEXT GENE ASTAIRE?! I AGREE, TINA!
TINA ALWAYS EVALUATES A STUDENT'S POTENTIAL BEFORE INSTRUCTION BEGINS! THAT WAS THE FREEBIE, AND IT ONLY COSTS FIFTEEN CLAMS A WEEK TO CONTINUE!
FIFTEEN CLAMS? GAWRSH! WITH THUH BEACH ALL THUH WAY ACROSS TOWN...
THAT'S ALL RIGHT! YOU CAN WORK HERE AS A DANCE-SHOE SALESMAN IN EXCHANGE FOR LESSONS! TALENT LIKE YOURS SHOULDN'T GO TO WASTE!
WHAT'S GOING ON, MOTHER? THAT SWEET GUY HAS TWO LEFT FEET! NO AMOUNT OF LESSONS IS GOING TO CHANGE THAT!
QUIET, DEAR! HE'LL HEAR YOU!
?
?

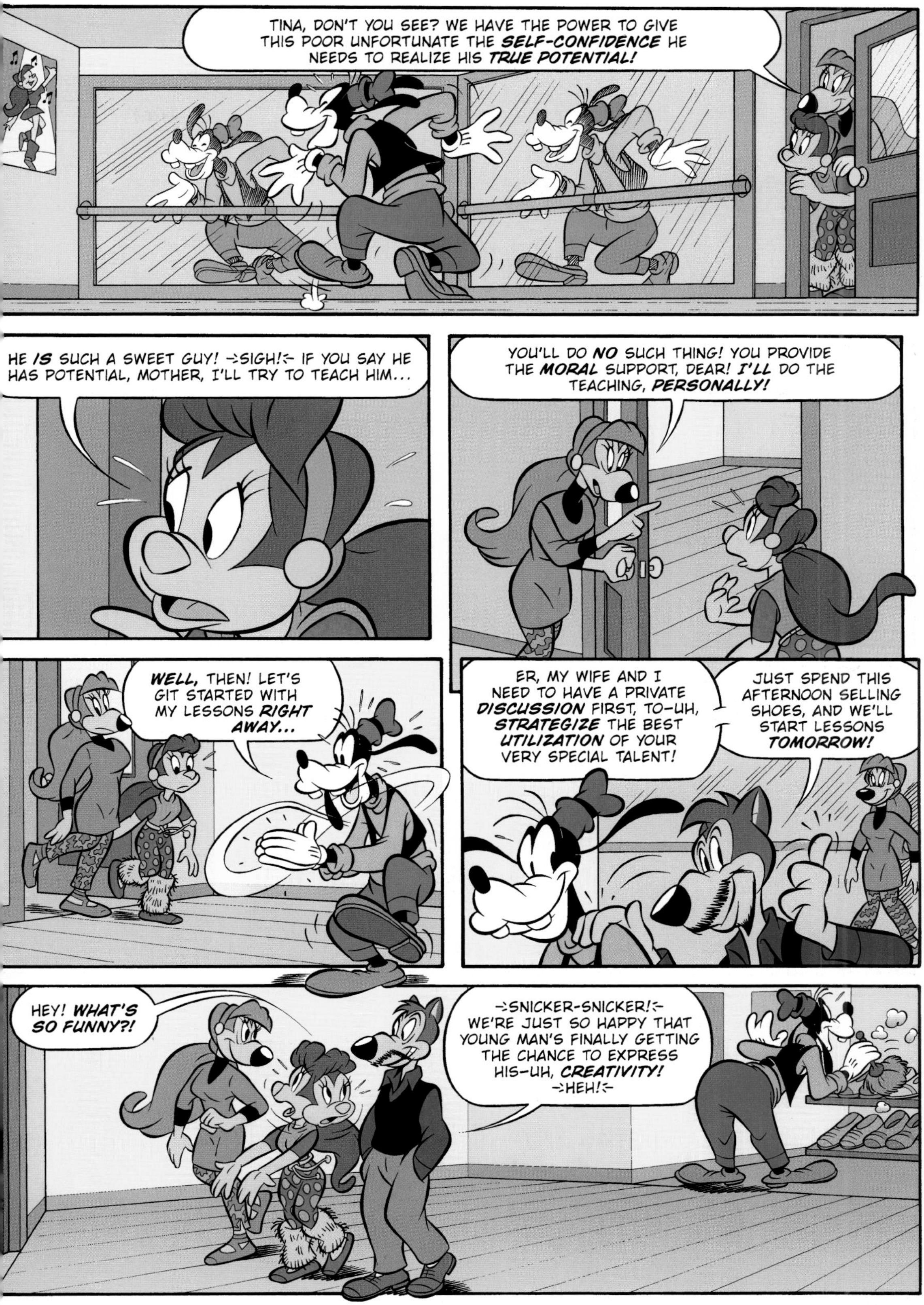
TINA, DON'T YOU SEE? WE HAVE THE POWER TO GIVE THIS POOR UNFORTUNATE THE SELF-CONFIDENCE HE NEEDS TO REALIZE HIS TRUE POTENTIAL!
HE IS SUCH A SWEET GUY! ~SIGH!~ IF YOU SAY HE HAS POTENTIAL, MOTHER, I'LL TRY TO TEACH HIM...
YOU'LL DO NO SUCH THING! YOU PROVIDE THE MORAL SUPPORT, DEAR! I'LL DO THE TEACHING, PERSONALLY!
WELL, THEN! LET'S GIT STARTED WITH MY LESSONS RIGHT AWAY...
ER, MY WIFE AND I NEED TO HAVE A PRIVATE DISCUSSION FIRST, TO-UH, STRATEGIZE THE BEST UTILIZATION OF YOUR VERY SPECIAL TALENT!
JUST SPEND THIS AFTERNOON SELLING SHOES, AND WE'LL START LESSONS TOMORROW!
HEY! WHAT'S SO FUNNY?!
~SNICKER-SNICKER!~ WE'RE JUST SO HAPPY THAT YOUNG MAN'S FINALLY GETTING THE CHANCE TO EXPRESS HIS-UH, CREATIVITY! ~HEH!~

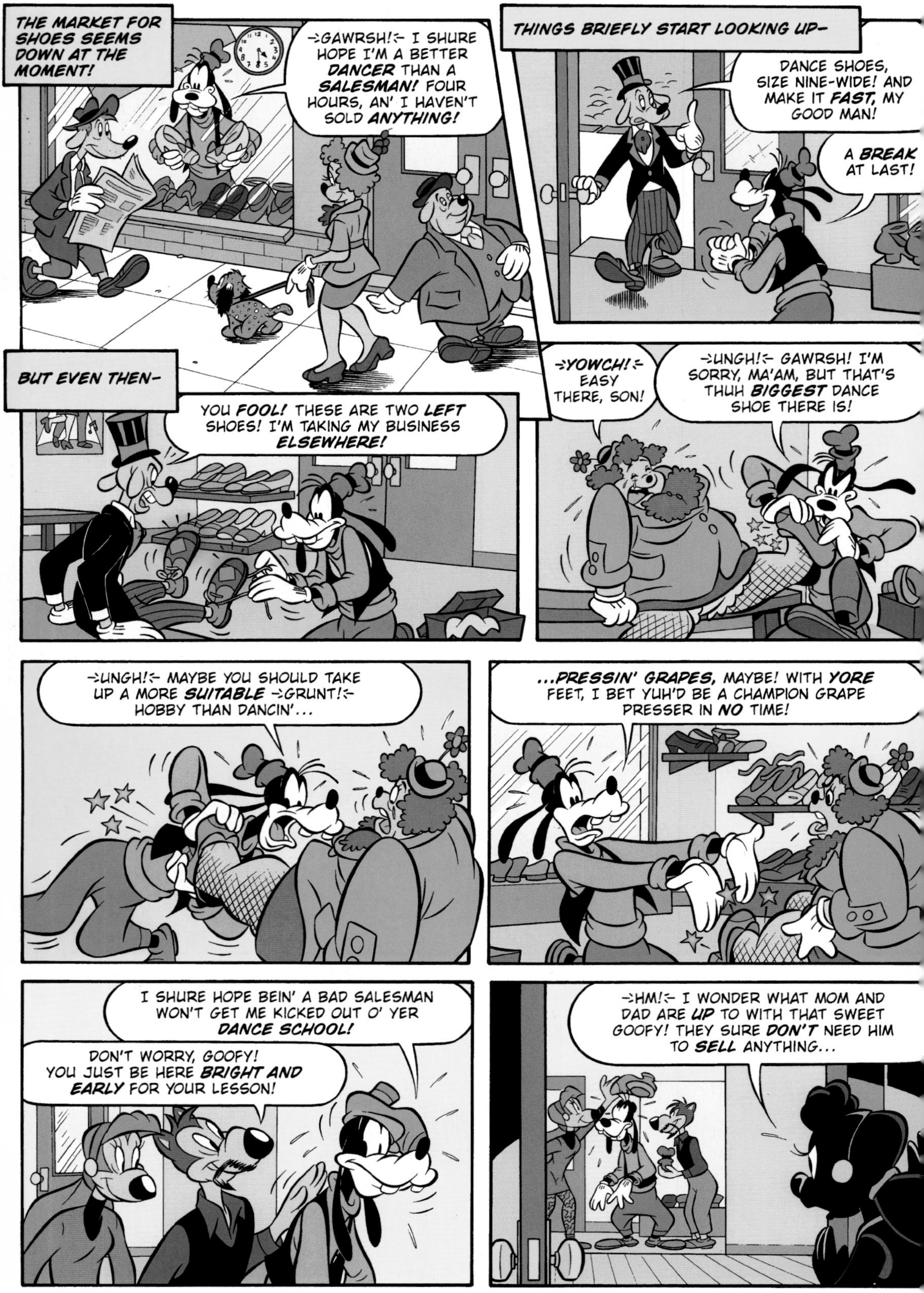
THE MARKET FOR SHOES SEEMS DOWN AT THE MOMENT!
-GAWRSH!- I SHURE HOPE I'M A BETTER DANCER THAN A SALESMAN! FOUR HOURS, AN' I HAVEN'T SOLD ANYTHING!
THINGS BRIEFLY START LOOKING UP-
DANCE SHOES, SIZE NINE-WIDE! AND MAKE IT FAST, MY GOOD MAN!
A BREAK AT LAST!
BUT EVEN THEN-
YOU FOOL! THESE ARE TWO LEFT SHOES! I'M TAKING MY BUSINESS ELSEWHERE!
-YOWCH!- EASY THERE, SON!
-UNGH!- GAWRSH! I'M SORRY, MA'AM, BUT THAT'S THUH BIGGEST DANCE SHOE THERE IS!
-UNGH!- MAYBE YOU SHOULD TAKE UP A MORE SUITABLE -GRUNT!- HOBBY THAN DANCIN'...
...PRESSIN' GRAPES, MAYBE! WITH YORE FEET, I BET YUH'D BE A CHAMPION GRAPE PRESSER IN NO TIME!
I SHURE HOPE BEIN' A BAD SALESMAN WON'T GET ME KICKED OUT O' YER DANCE SCHOOL!
DON'T WORRY, GOOFY! YOU JUST BE HERE BRIGHT AND EARLY FOR YOUR LESSON!
-HM!- I WONDER WHAT MOM AND DAD ARE UP TO WITH THAT SWEET GOOFY! THEY SURE DON'T NEED HIM TO SELL ANYTHING...

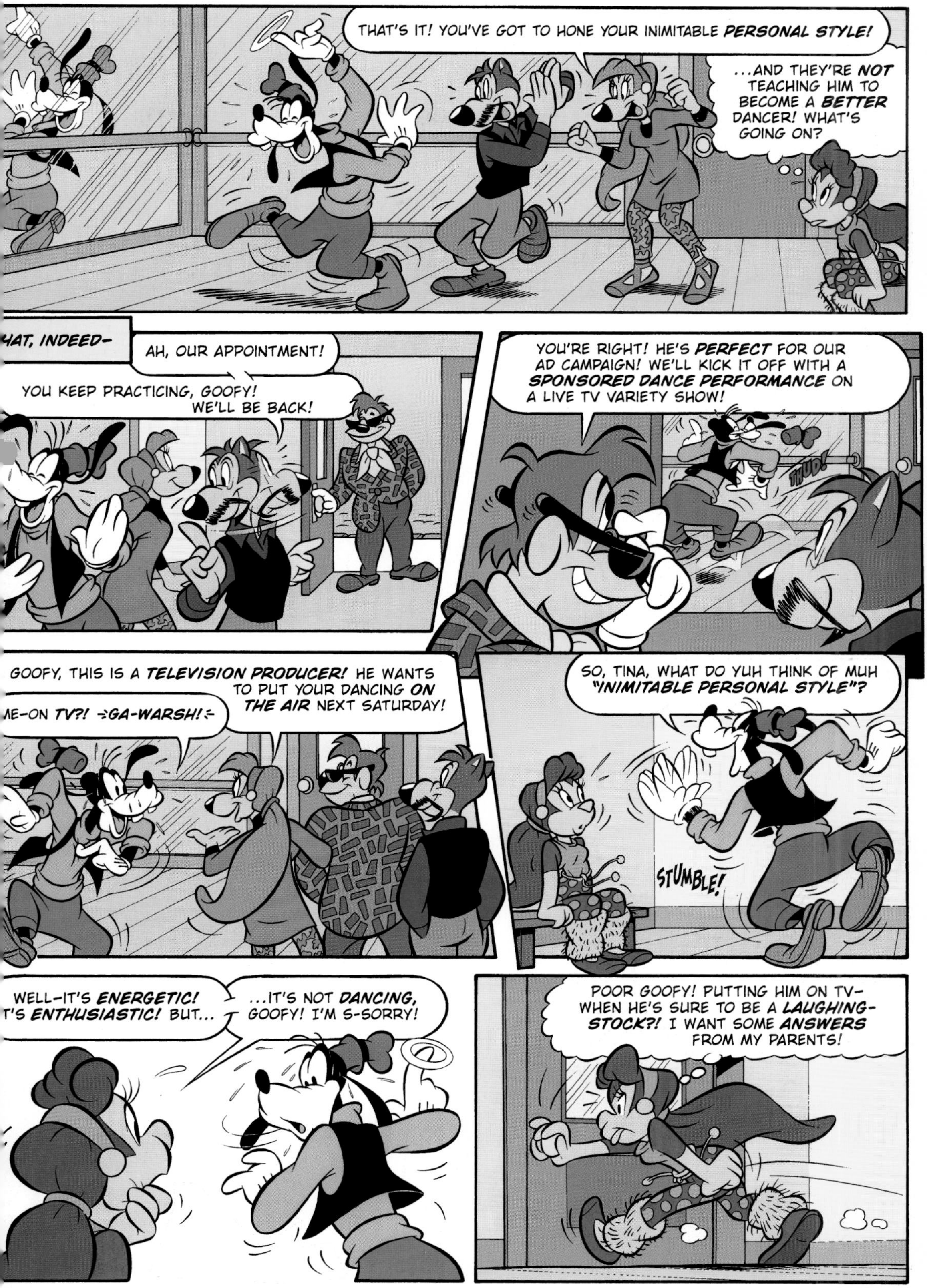
THAT'S IT! YOU'VE GOT TO HONE YOUR INIMITABLE PERSONAL STYLE!
...AND THEY'RE NOT TEACHING HIM TO BECOME A BETTER DANCER! WHAT'S GOING ON?
HAT, INDEED-
AH, OUR APPOINTMENT!
YOU KEEP PRACTICING, GOOFY! WE'LL BE BACK!
YOU'RE RIGHT! HE'S PERFECT FOR OUR AD CAMPAIGN! WE'LL KICK IT OFF WITH A SPONSORED DANCE PERFORMANCE ON A LIVE TV VARIETY SHOW!
THUD!
GOOFY, THIS IS A TELEVISION PRODUCER! HE WANTS TO PUT YOUR DANCING ON THE AIR NEXT SATURDAY!
ME-ON TV?! GA-WARSH!
SO, TINA, WHAT DO YUH THINK OF MUH "INIMITABLE PERSONAL STYLE"?
STUMBLE!
WELL-IT'S ENERGETIC! T'S ENTHUSIASTIC! BUT...
...IT'S NOT DANCING, GOOFY! I'M S-SORRY!
POOR GOOFY! PUTTING HIM ON TV-WHEN HE'S SURE TO BE A LAUGHING-STOCK?! I WANT SOME ANSWERS FROM MY PARENTS!

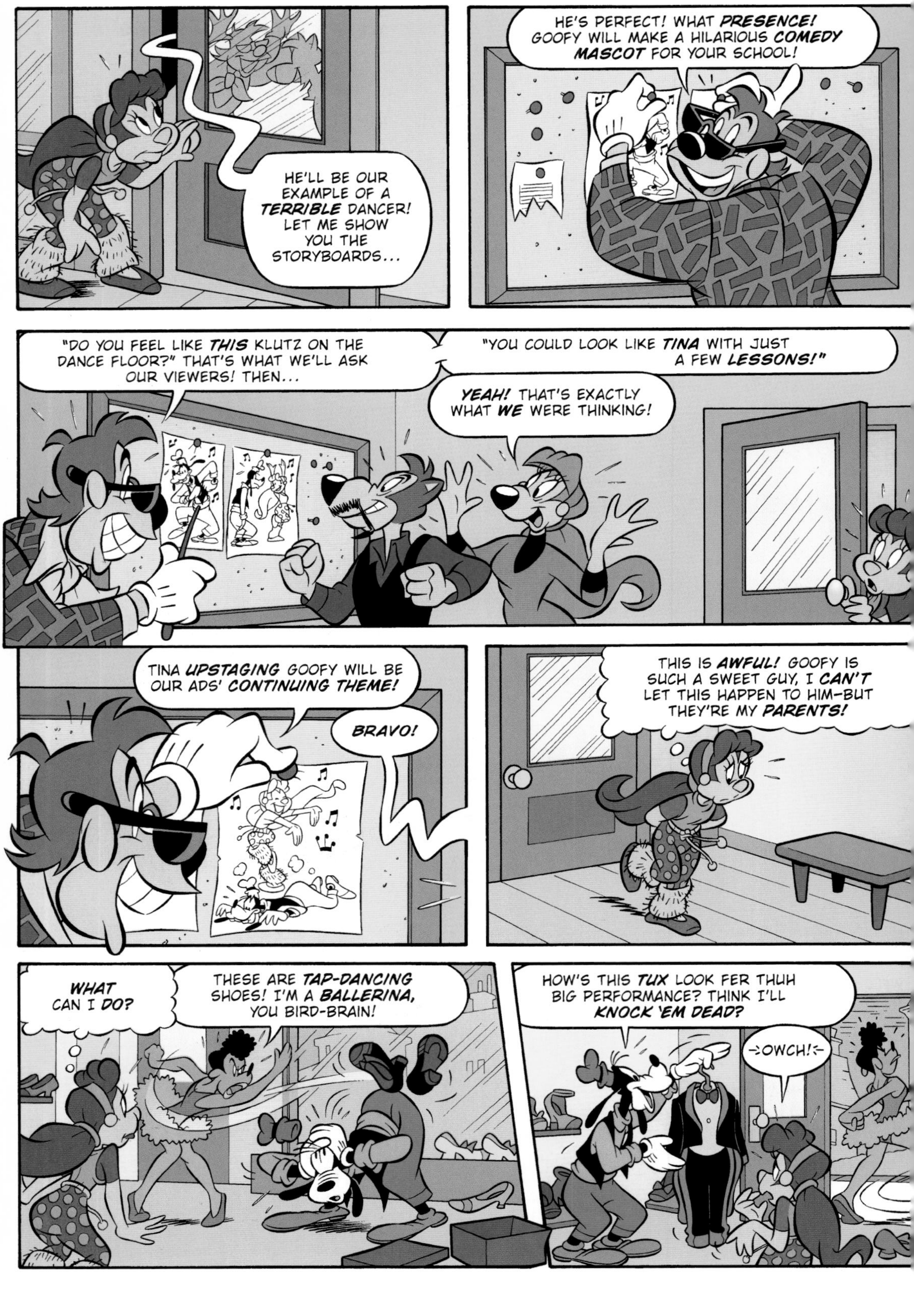
HE'LL BE OUR EXAMPLE OF A TERRIBLE DANCER! LET ME SHOW YOU THE STORYBOARDS...
HE'S PERFECT! WHAT PRESENCE! GOOFY WILL MAKE A HILARIOUS COMEDY MASCOT FOR YOUR SCHOOL!
"DO YOU FEEL LIKE THIS KLUTZ ON THE DANCE FLOOR?" THAT'S WHAT WE'LL ASK OUR VIEWERS! THEN...
"YOU COULD LOOK LIKE TINA WITH JUST A FEW LESSONS!"
YEAH! THAT'S EXACTLY WHAT WE WERE THINKING!
TINA UPSTAGING GOOFY WILL BE OUR ADS' CONTINUING THEME!
BRAVO!
THIS IS AWFUL! GOOFY IS SUCH A SWEET GUY, I CAN'T LET THIS HAPPEN TO HIM–BUT THEY'RE MY PARENTS!
WHAT CAN I DO?
THESE ARE TAP-DANCING SHOES! I'M A BALLERINA, YOU BIRD-BRAIN!
HOW'S THIS TUX LOOK FER THUH BIG PERFORMANCE? THINK I'LL KNOCK 'EM DEAD?
OWCH!

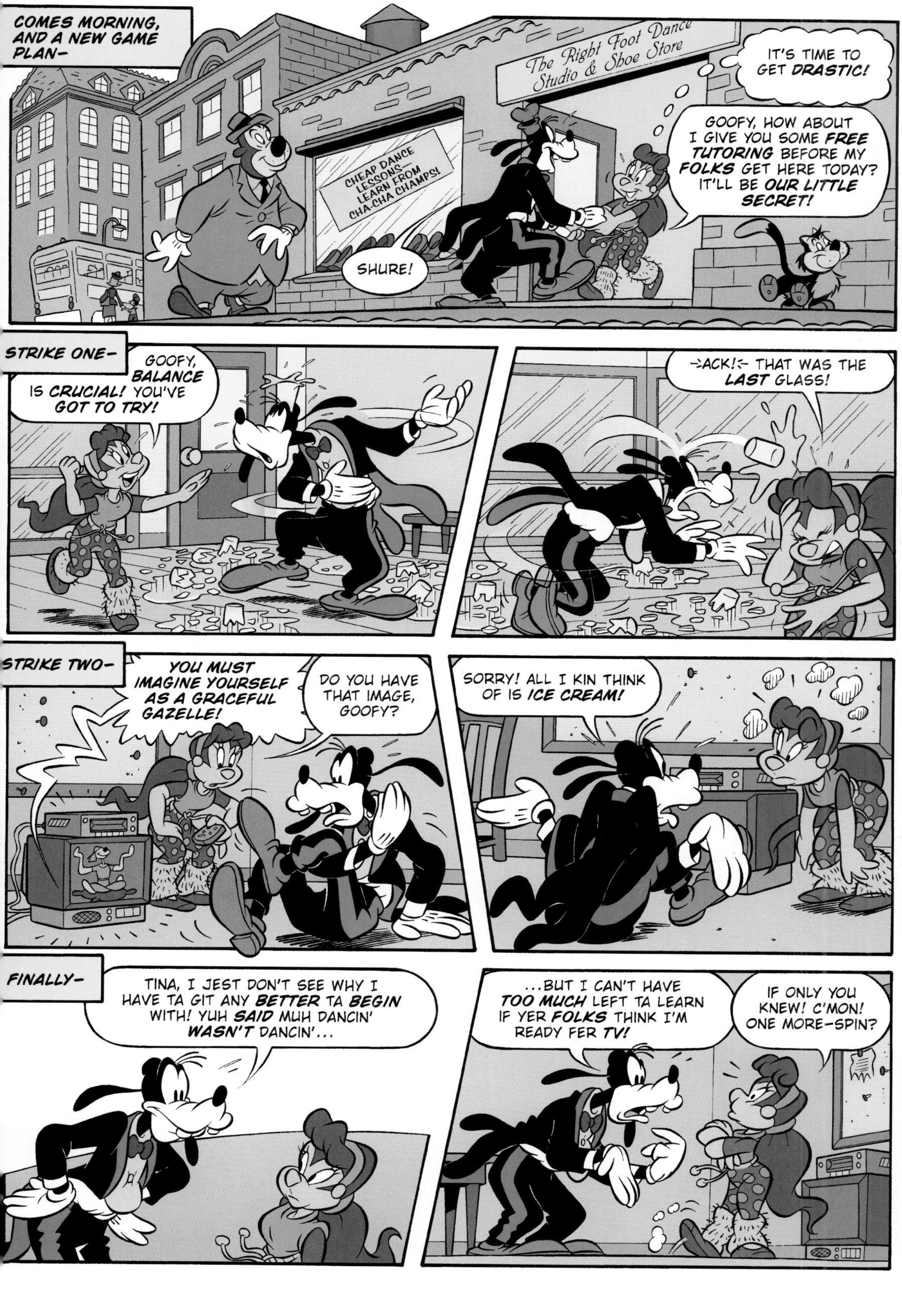
COMES MORNING, AND A NEW GAME PLAN—
The Right Foot Dance Studio & Shoe Store
CHEAP DANCE LESSONS— LEARN FROM CHA-CHA CHAMPS!
IT'S TIME TO GET DRASTIC!
GOOFY, HOW ABOUT I GIVE YOU SOME FREE TUTORING BEFORE MY FOLKS GET HERE TODAY? IT'LL BE OUR LITTLE SECRET!
SHURE!
STRIKE ONE—
GOOFY, BALANCE IS CRUCIAL! YOU'VE GOT TO TRY!
→ACK!← THAT WAS THE LAST GLASS!
STRIKE TWO—
YOU MUST IMAGINE YOURSELF AS A GRACEFUL GAZELLE!
DO YOU HAVE THAT IMAGE, GOOFY?
SORRY! ALL I KIN THINK OF IS ICE CREAM!
FINALLY—
TINA, I JEST DON'T SEE WHY I HAVE TA GIT ANY BETTER TA BEGIN WITH! YUH SAID MUH DANCIN' WASN'T DANCIN'...
...BUT I CAN'T HAVE TOO MUCH LEFT TA LEARN IF YER FOLKS THINK I'M READY FER TV!
IF ONLY YOU KNEW! C'MON! ONE MORE-SPIN?

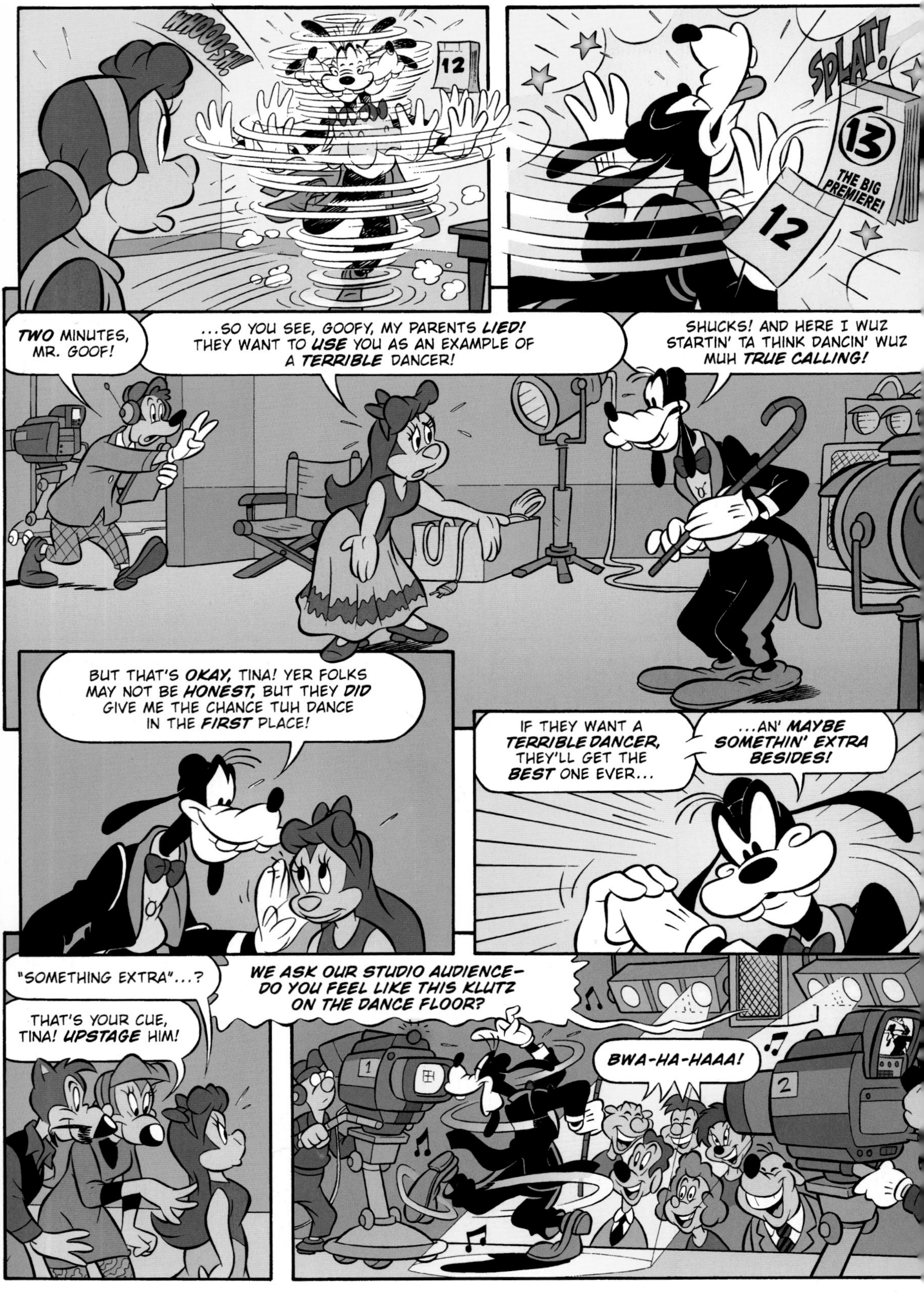
WHOOOSH!
12
SPLAT!
13
THE BIG PREMIERE!
12
TWO MINUTES, MR. GOOF!
...SO YOU SEE, GOOFY, MY PARENTS LIED! THEY WANT TO USE YOU AS AN EXAMPLE OF A TERRIBLE DANCER!
SHUCKS! AND HERE I WUZ STARTIN' TA THINK DANCIN' WUZ MUH TRUE CALLING!
BUT THAT'S OKAY, TINA! YER FOLKS MAY NOT BE HONEST, BUT THEY DID GIVE ME THE CHANCE TUH DANCE IN THE FIRST PLACE!
IF THEY WANT A TERRIBLE DANCER, THEY'LL GET THE BEST ONE EVER...
...AN' MAYBE SOMETHIN' EXTRA BESIDES!
"SOMETHING EXTRA"...?
THAT'S YOUR CUE, TINA! UPSTAGE HIM!
WE ASK OUR STUDIO AUDIENCE- DO YOU FEEL LIKE THIS KLUTZ ON THE DANCE FLOOR?
BWA-HA-HAAA!
1
2

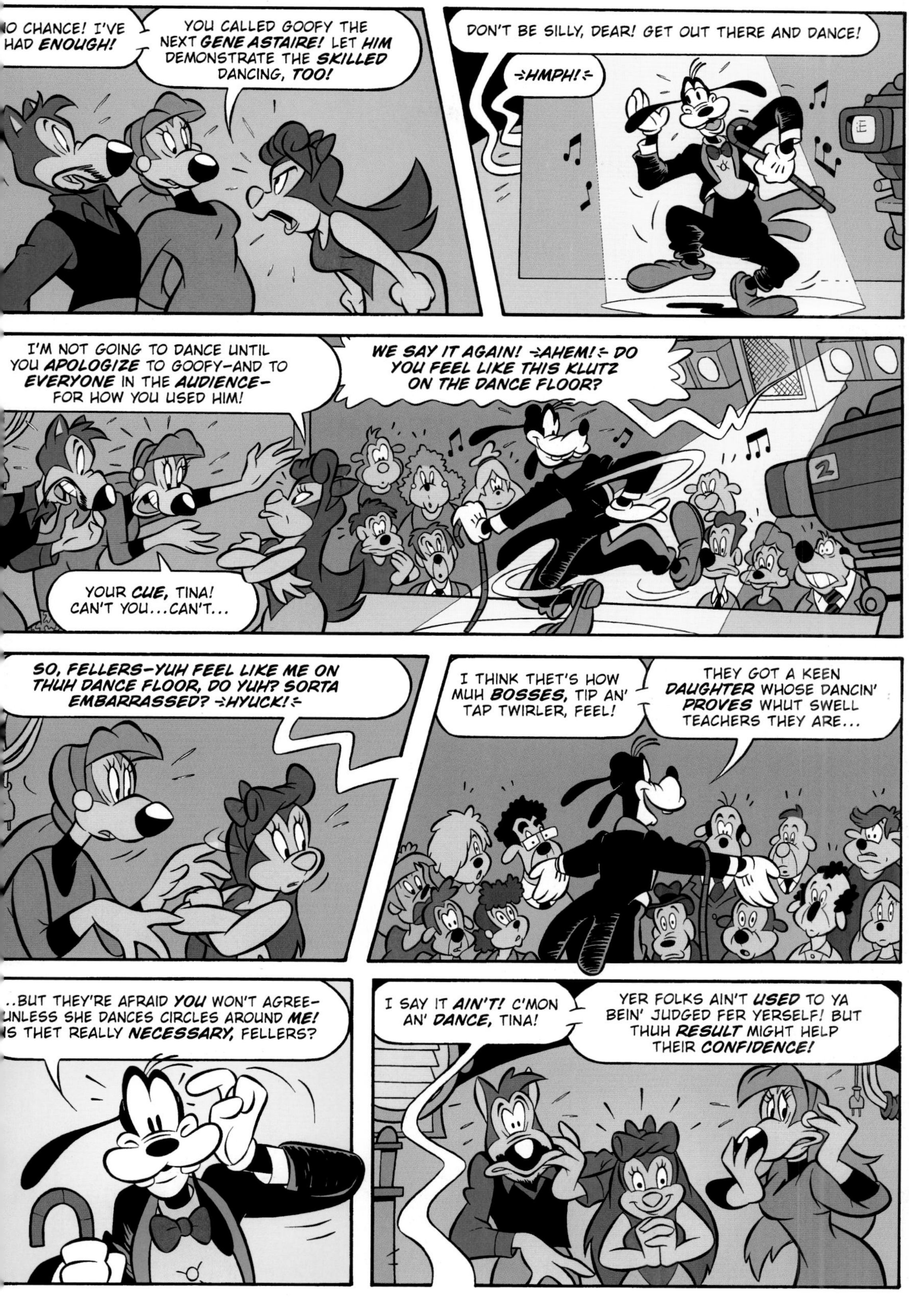

O CHANCE! I'VE HAD ENOUGH!
YOU CALLED GOOFY THE NEXT GENE ASTAIRE! LET HIM DEMONSTRATE THE SKILLED DANCING, TOO!
DON'T BE SILLY, DEAR! GET OUT THERE AND DANCE!
HMPH!
I'M NOT GOING TO DANCE UNTIL YOU APOLOGIZE TO GOOFY—AND TO EVERYONE IN THE AUDIENCE—FOR HOW YOU USED HIM!
WE SAY IT AGAIN! AHEM! DO YOU FEEL LIKE THIS KLUTZ ON THE DANCE FLOOR?
YOUR CUE, TINA! CAN'T YOU...CAN'T...
SO, FELLERS—YUH FEEL LIKE ME ON THUH DANCE FLOOR, DO YUH? SORTA EMBARRASSED? HYUCK!
I THINK THET'S HOW MUH BOSSES, TIP AN' TAP TWIRLER, FEEL!
THEY GOT A KEEN DAUGHTER WHOSE DANCIN' PROVES WHUT SWELL TEACHERS THEY ARE...
..BUT THEY'RE AFRAID YOU WON'T AGREE—UNLESS SHE DANCES CIRCLES AROUND ME! S THET REALLY NECESSARY, FELLERS?
I SAY IT AIN'T! C'MON AN' DANCE, TINA!
YER FOLKS AIN'T USED TO YA BEIN' JUDGED FER YERSELF! BUT THUH RESULT MIGHT HELP THEIR CONFIDENCE!

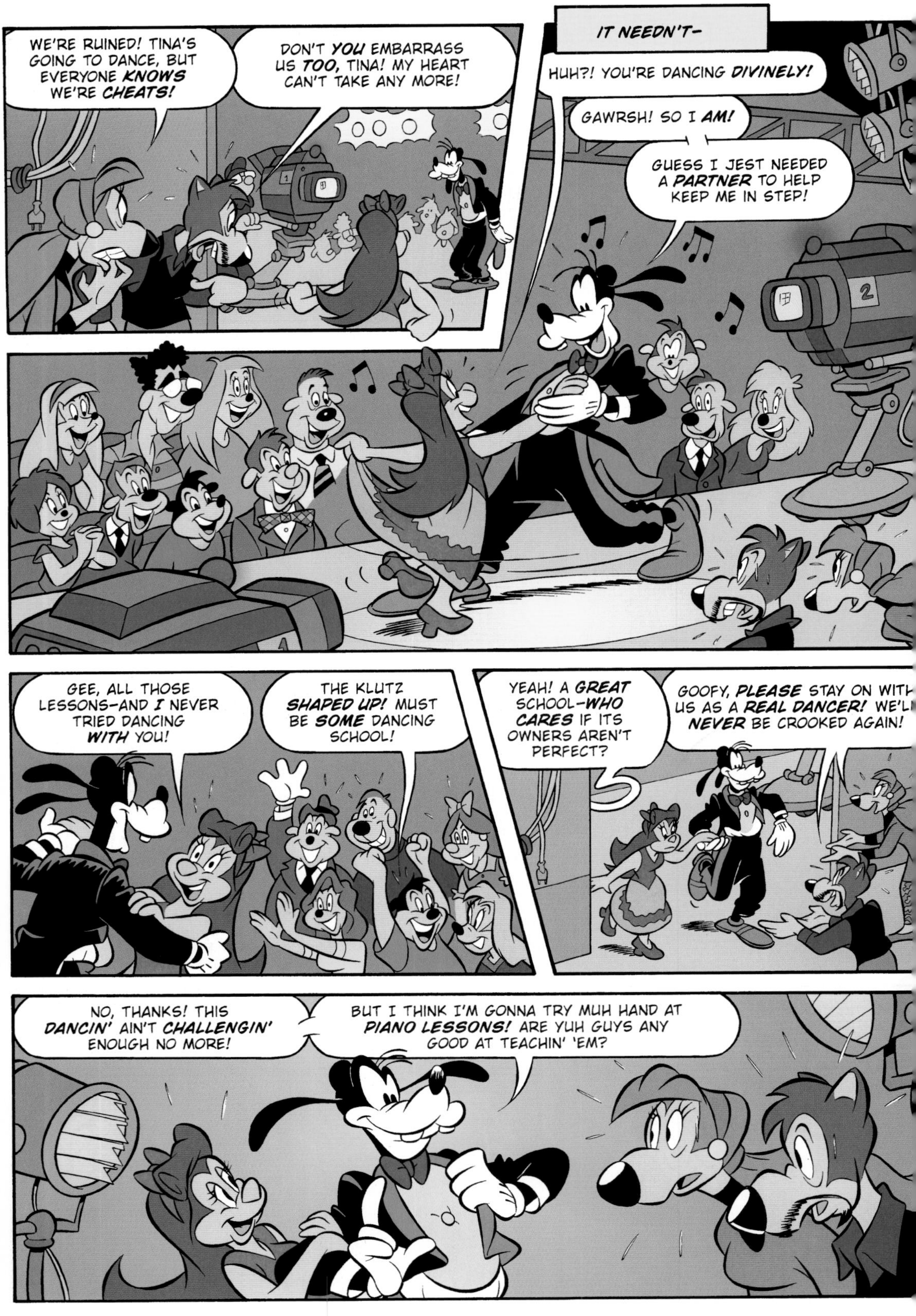
WE'RE RUINED! TINA'S GOING TO DANCE, BUT EVERYONE KNOWS WE'RE CHEATS!
DON'T YOU EMBARRASS US TOO, TINA! MY HEART CAN'T TAKE ANY MORE!
IT NEEDN'T–
HUH?! YOU'RE DANCING DIVINELY!
GAWRSH! SO I AM!
GUESS I JEST NEEDED A PARTNER TO HELP KEEP ME IN STEP!
GEE, ALL THOSE LESSONS–AND I NEVER TRIED DANCING WITH YOU!
THE KLUTZ SHAPED UP! MUST BE SOME DANCING SCHOOL!
YEAH! A GREAT SCHOOL–WHO CARES IF ITS OWNERS AREN'T PERFECT?
GOOFY, PLEASE STAY ON WITH US AS A REAL DANCER! WE'LL NEVER BE CROOKED AGAIN!
NO, THANKS! THIS DANCIN' AIN'T CHALLENGIN' ENOUGH NO MORE!
BUT I THINK I'M GONNA TRY MUH HAND AT PIANO LESSONS! ARE YUH GUYS ANY GOOD AT TEACHIN' 'EM?

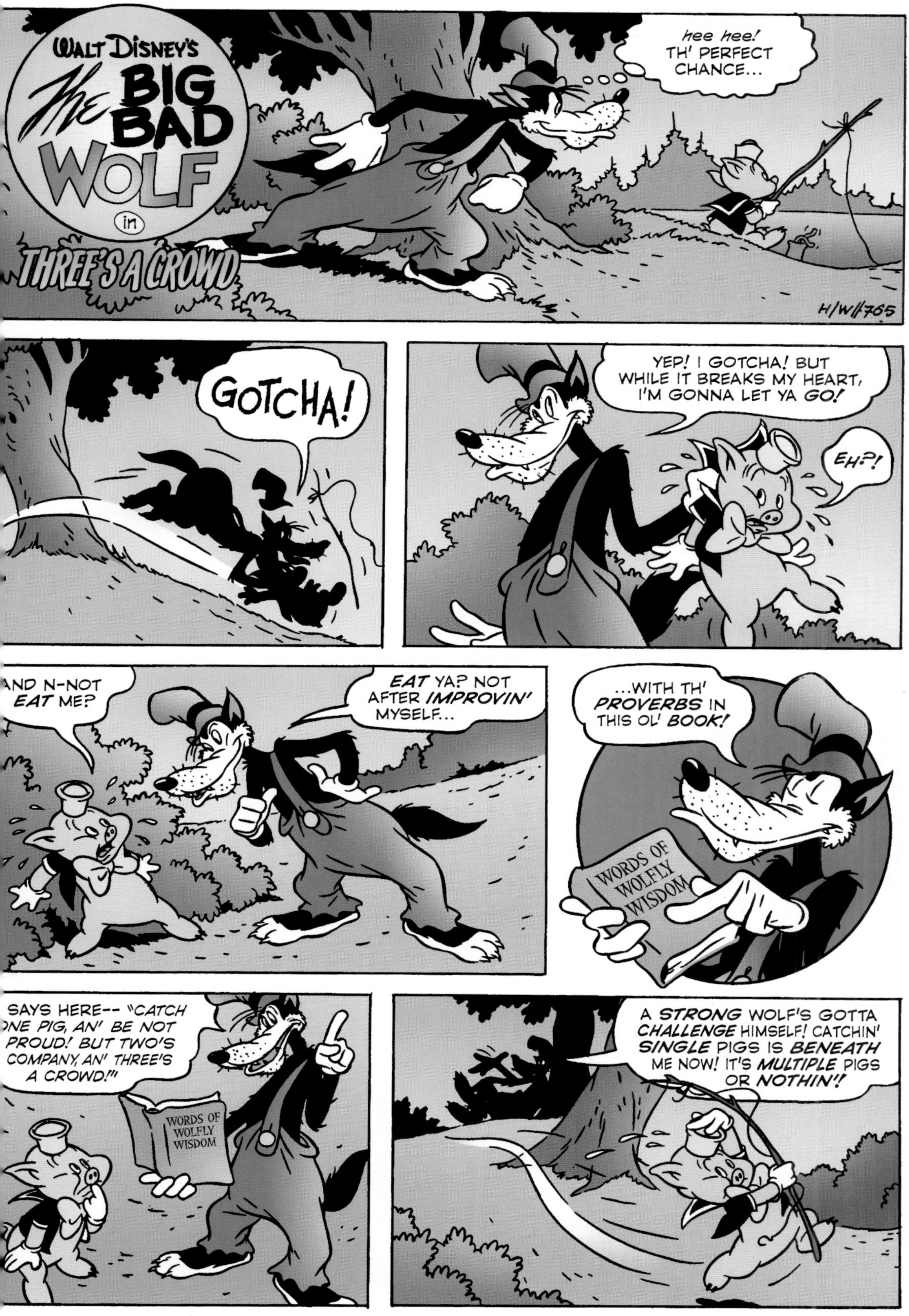
WALT DISNEY'S
THE BIG BAD WOLF
in
THREE'S A CROWD
hee hee! TH' PERFECT CHANCE...
H/W//765
GOTCHA!
YEP! I GOTCHA! BUT WHILE IT BREAKS MY HEART, I'M GONNA LET YA GO!
EH?!
AND N-NOT EAT ME?
EAT YA? NOT AFTER IMPROVIN' MYSELF...
...WITH TH' PROVERBS IN THIS OL' BOOK!
WORDS OF WOLFLY WISDOM
SAYS HERE-- "CATCH ONE PIG, AN' BE NOT PROUD! BUT TWO'S COMPANY, AN' THREE'S A CROWD!"
WORDS OF WOLFLY WISDOM
A STRONG WOLF'S GOTTA CHALLENGE HIMSELF! CATCHIN' SINGLE PIGS IS BENEATH ME NOW! IT'S MULTIPLE PIGS OR NOTHIN'!

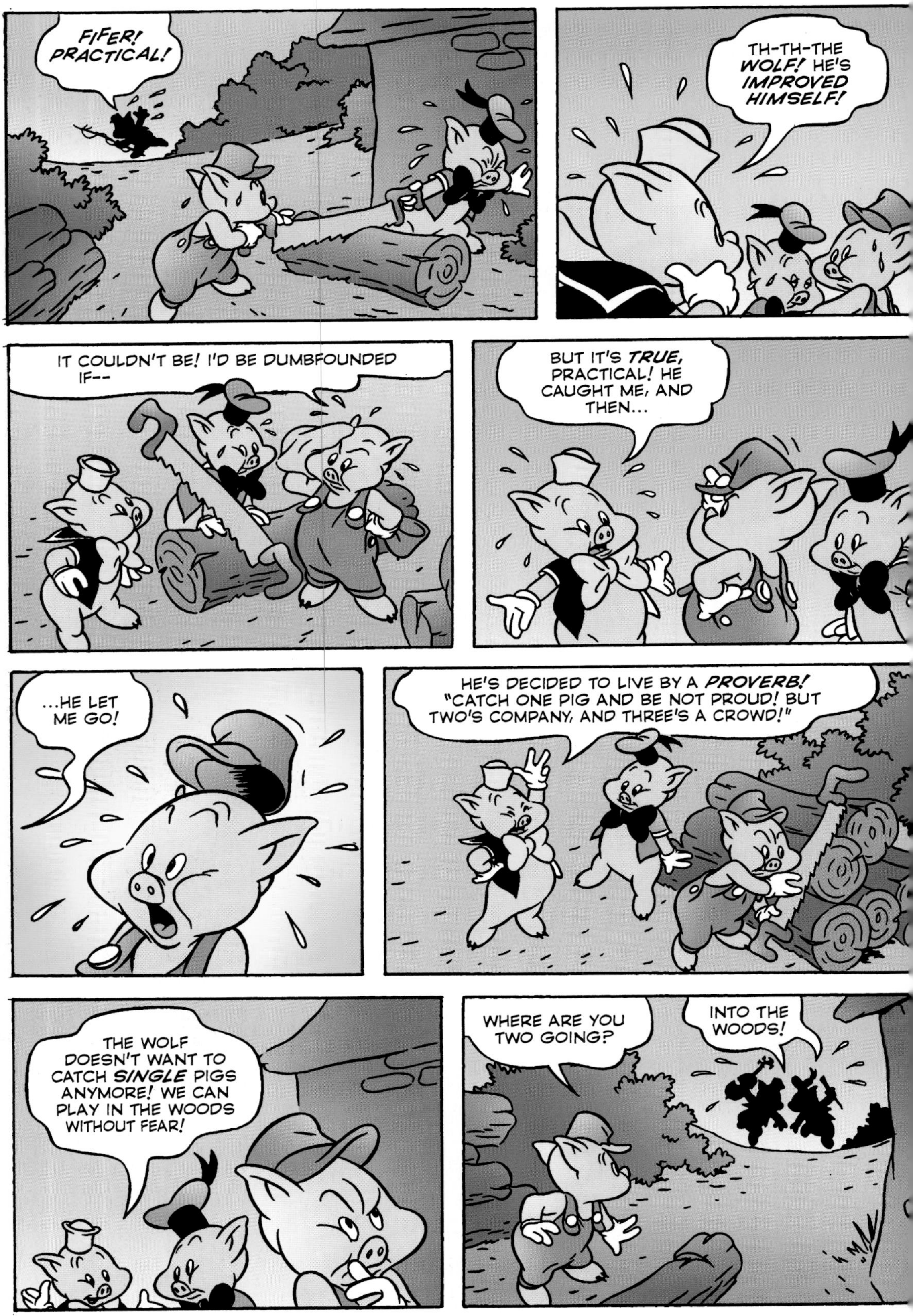
FIFER! PRACTICAL!
TH-TH-THE WOLF! HE'S IMPROVED HIMSELF!
IT COULDN'T BE! I'D BE DUMBFOUNDED IF--
BUT IT'S TRUE, PRACTICAL! HE CAUGHT ME, AND THEN...
...HE LET ME GO!
HE'S DECIDED TO LIVE BY A PROVERB! "CATCH ONE PIG AND BE NOT PROUD! BUT TWO'S COMPANY, AND THREE'S A CROWD!"
THE WOLF DOESN'T WANT TO CATCH SINGLE PIGS ANYMORE! WE CAN PLAY IN THE WOODS WITHOUT FEAR!
WHERE ARE YOU TWO GOING?
INTO THE WOODS!

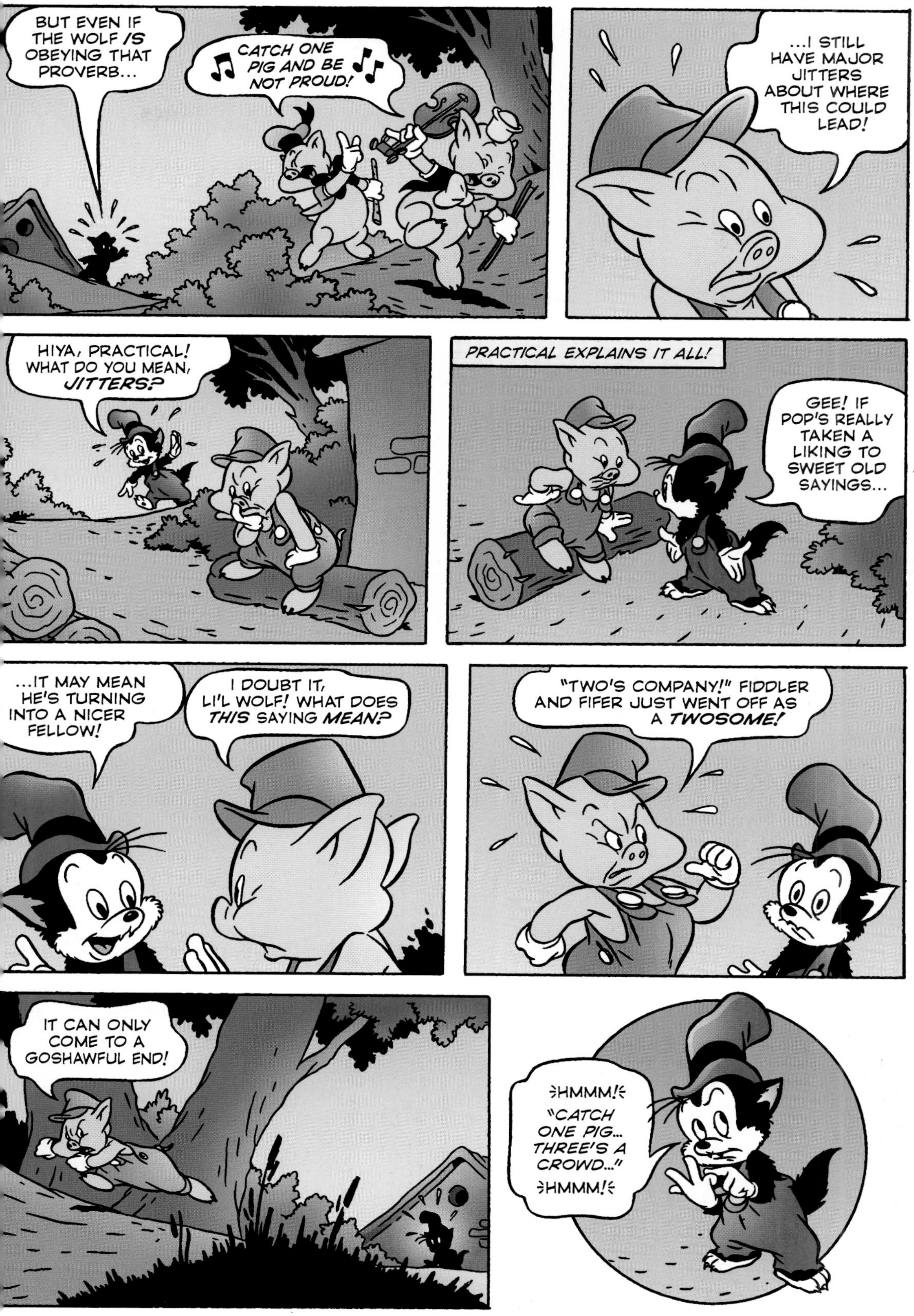
BUT EVEN IF THE WOLF *IS* OBEYING THAT PROVERB...
CATCH ONE PIG AND BE NOT PROUD!
...I STILL HAVE MAJOR JITTERS ABOUT WHERE THIS COULD LEAD!
HIYA, PRACTICAL! WHAT DO YOU MEAN, *JITTERS?*
PRACTICAL EXPLAINS IT ALL!
GEE! IF POP'S REALLY TAKEN A LIKING TO SWEET OLD SAYINGS...
...IT MAY MEAN HE'S TURNING INTO A NICER FELLOW!
I DOUBT IT, LI'L WOLF! WHAT DOES *THIS* SAYING *MEAN?*
"TWO'S COMPANY!" FIDDLER AND FIFER JUST WENT OFF AS A *TWOSOME!*
IT CAN ONLY COME TO A GOSHAWFUL END!
HMMM!
"CATCH ONE PIG... THREE'S A CROWD..."
HMMM!

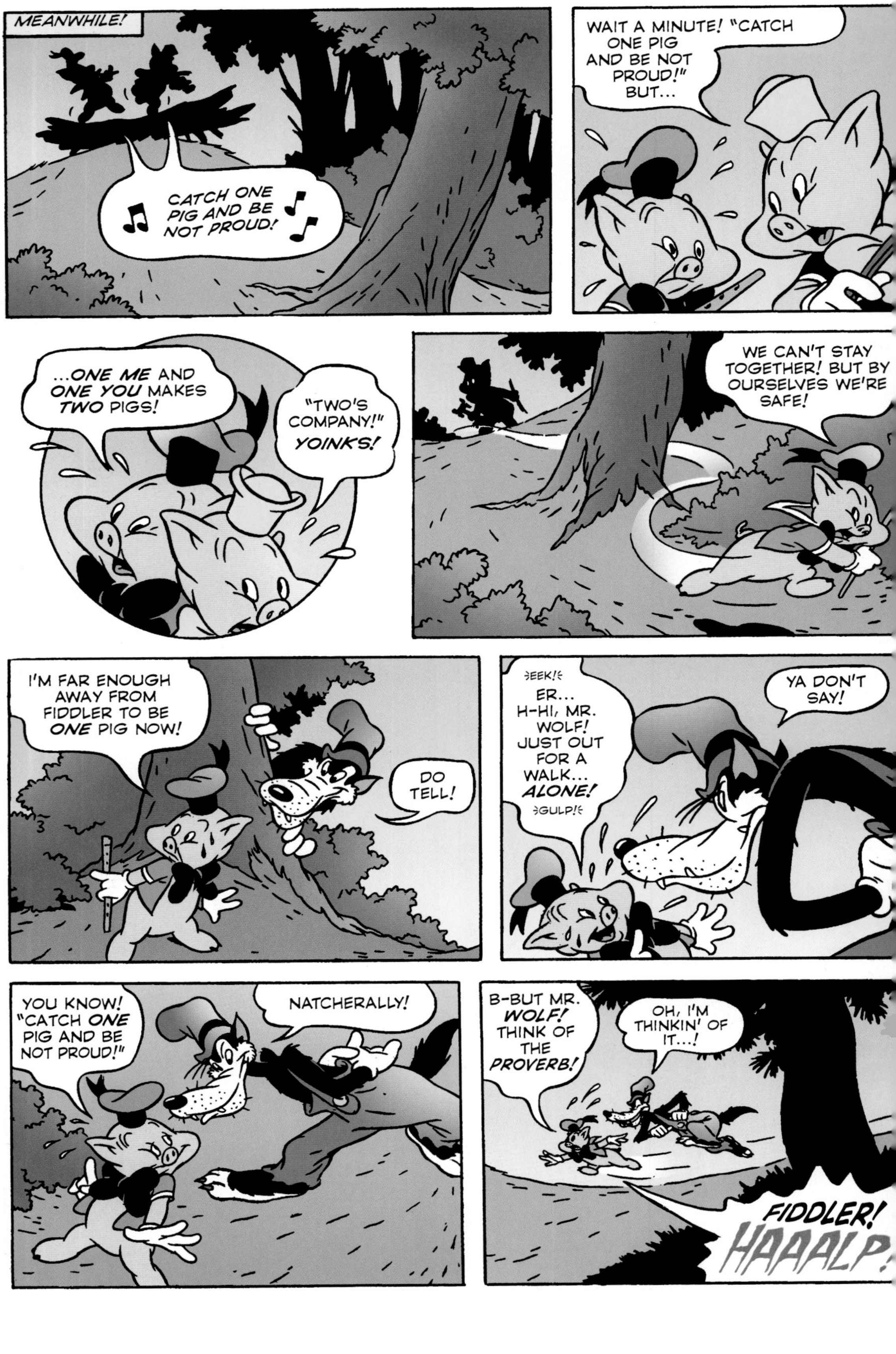
MEANWHILE!
CATCH ONE PIG AND BE NOT PROUD!
WAIT A MINUTE! "CATCH ONE PIG AND BE NOT PROUD!" BUT...
...ONE ME AND ONE YOU MAKES TWO PIGS!
"TWO'S COMPANY!" YOINKS!
WE CAN'T STAY TOGETHER! BUT BY OURSELVES WE'RE SAFE!
I'M FAR ENOUGH AWAY FROM FIDDLER TO BE ONE PIG NOW!
DO TELL!
EEK!
ER... H-HI, MR. WOLF! JUST OUT FOR A WALK... ALONE!
GULP!
YA DON'T SAY!
YOU KNOW! "CATCH ONE PIG AND BE NOT PROUD!"
NATCHERALLY!
B-BUT MR. WOLF! THINK OF THE PROVERB!
OH, I'M THINKIN' OF IT...!
FIDDLER! HAAALP!

HEADS UP! FIDDLER!

CATCH ONE PIG AN' BE NOT PROUD!

BUT TWO'S COMPANY... *hee hee!*

RUN FOR IT!

PRACTICAL!

AN' *THREE'S...*

...A *CROWD!* ⸲SNICKER!⸰

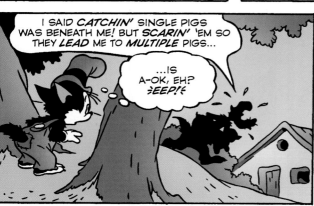

I SAID *CATCHIN'* SINGLE PIGS WAS BENEATH ME! BUT *SCARIN'* 'EM SO THEY *LEAD* ME TO *MULTIPLE* PIGS...

...IS A-OK, EH? ⸲EEP!⸰

PRACTICAL WAS RIGHT! THAT PROVERB DIDN'T CHANGE POP AT ALL!

BUT AS LONG AS HE'S GOT IT ON HIS *MIND*... I MIGHT STILL HAVE *ONE* CHANCE...

COSTUMES

...TO SAVE MY PIGGY PALS! I *HOPE!*

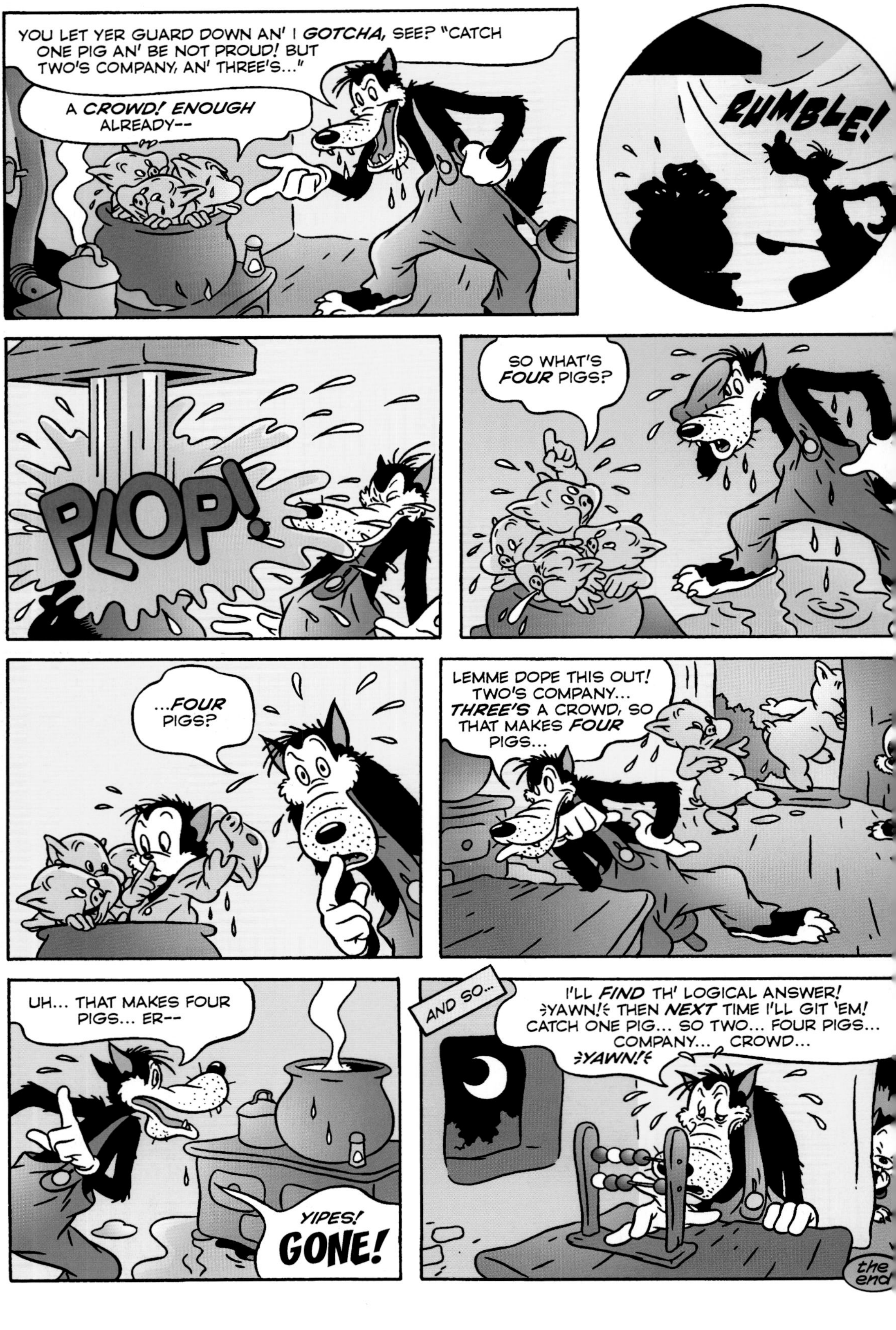

YOU LET YER GUARD DOWN AN' I GOTCHA, SEE? "CATCH ONE PIG AN' BE NOT PROUD! BUT TWO'S COMPANY, AN' THREE'S..."
A CROWD! ENOUGH ALREADY--
RUMBLE!
PLOP!
SO WHAT'S FOUR PIGS?
...FOUR PIGS?
LEMME DOPE THIS OUT! TWO'S COMPANY... THREE'S A CROWD, SO THAT MAKES FOUR PIGS...
UH... THAT MAKES FOUR PIGS... ER--
YIPES! GONE!
AND SO...
I'LL FIND TH' LOGICAL ANSWER! YAWN! THEN NEXT TIME I'LL GIT 'EM! CATCH ONE PIG... SO TWO... FOUR PIGS... COMPANY... CROWD...
YAWN!
the end

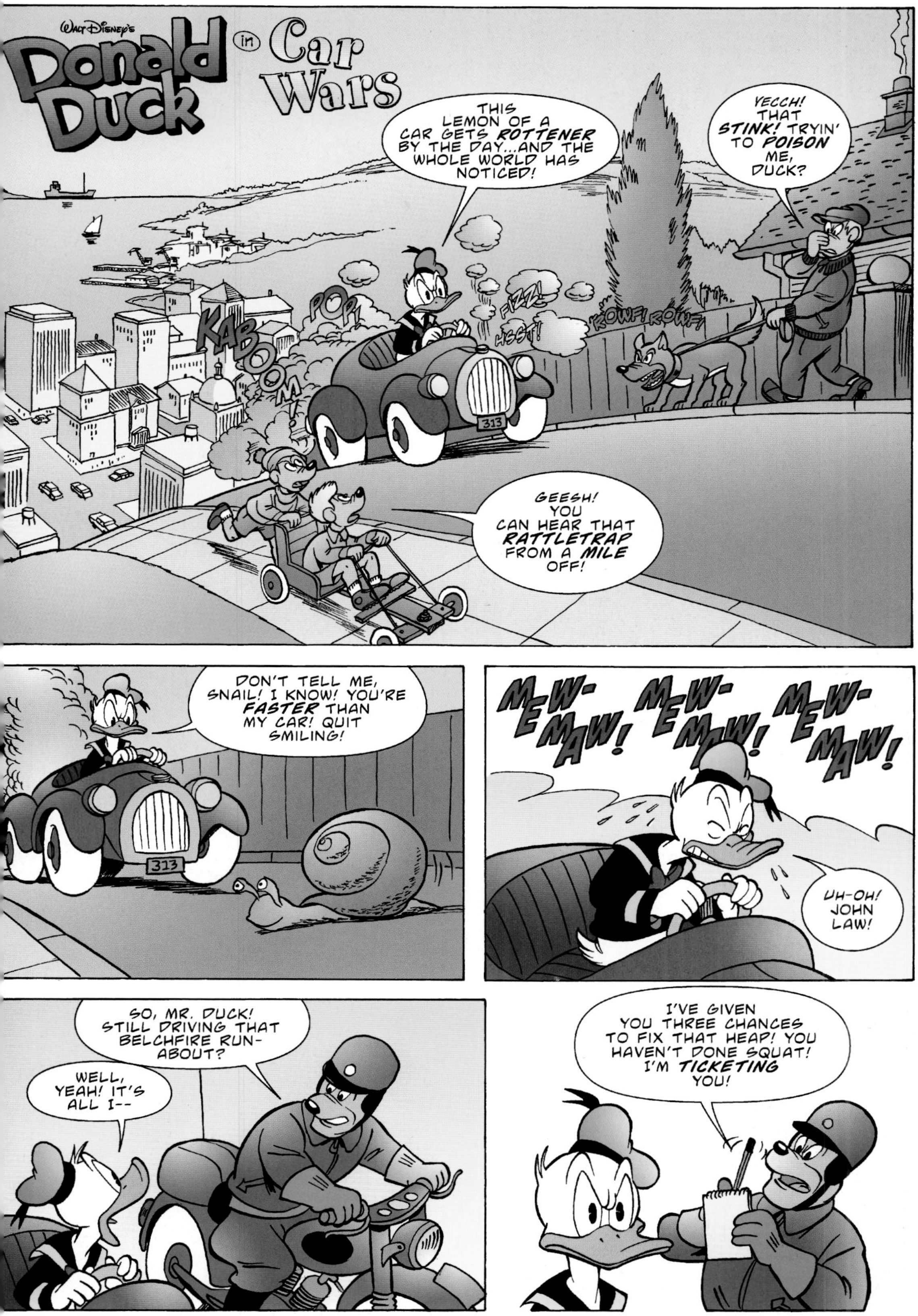
Walt Disney's
Donald Duck in Car Wars
THIS LEMON OF A CAR GETS ROTTENER BY THE DAY...AND THE WHOLE WORLD HAS NOTICED!
YECCH! THAT STINK! TRYIN' TO POISON ME, DUCK?
POP!
KABOOM!
FIZZ!
HSST!
ROWF! ROWF!
313
GEESH! YOU CAN HEAR THAT RATTLETRAP FROM A MILE OFF!
DON'T TELL ME, SNAIL! I KNOW! YOU'RE FASTER THAN MY CAR! QUIT SMILING!
313
MEW-EMAW! MEW-EMAW! MEW-EMAW!
UH-OH! JOHN LAW!
SO, MR. DUCK! STILL DRIVING THAT BELCHFIRE RUN-ABOUT?
WELL, YEAH! IT'S ALL I--
I'VE GIVEN YOU THREE CHANCES TO FIX THAT HEAP! YOU HAVEN'T DONE SQUAT! I'M TICKETING YOU!

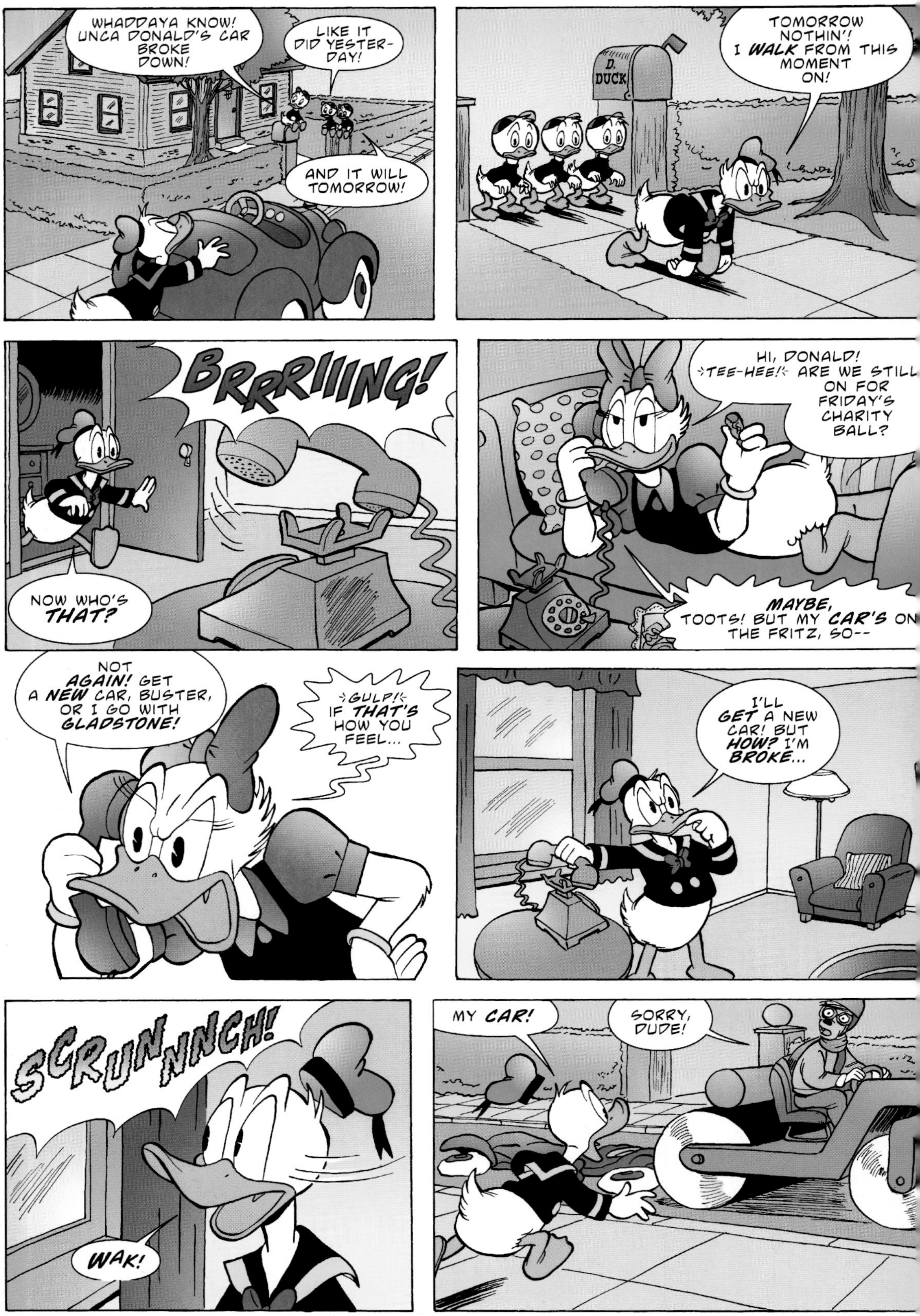
WHADDAYA KNOW! UNCA DONALD'S CAR BROKE DOWN!
LIKE IT DID YESTER-DAY!
AND IT WILL TOMORROW!
TOMORROW NOTHIN'! I WALK FROM THIS MOMENT ON!
D. DUCK
BRRRIIING!
NOW WHO'S THAT?
HI, DONALD! *TEE-HEE!* ARE WE STILL ON FOR FRIDAY'S CHARITY BALL?
MAYBE, TOOTS! BUT MY CAR'S ON THE FRITZ, SO--
NOT AGAIN! GET A NEW CAR, BUSTER, OR I GO WITH GLADSTONE!
GULP! IF THAT'S HOW YOU FEEL...
I'LL GET A NEW CAR! BUT HOW? I'M BROKE...
SCRUNNNCH!
WAK!
MY CAR!
SORRY, DUDE!

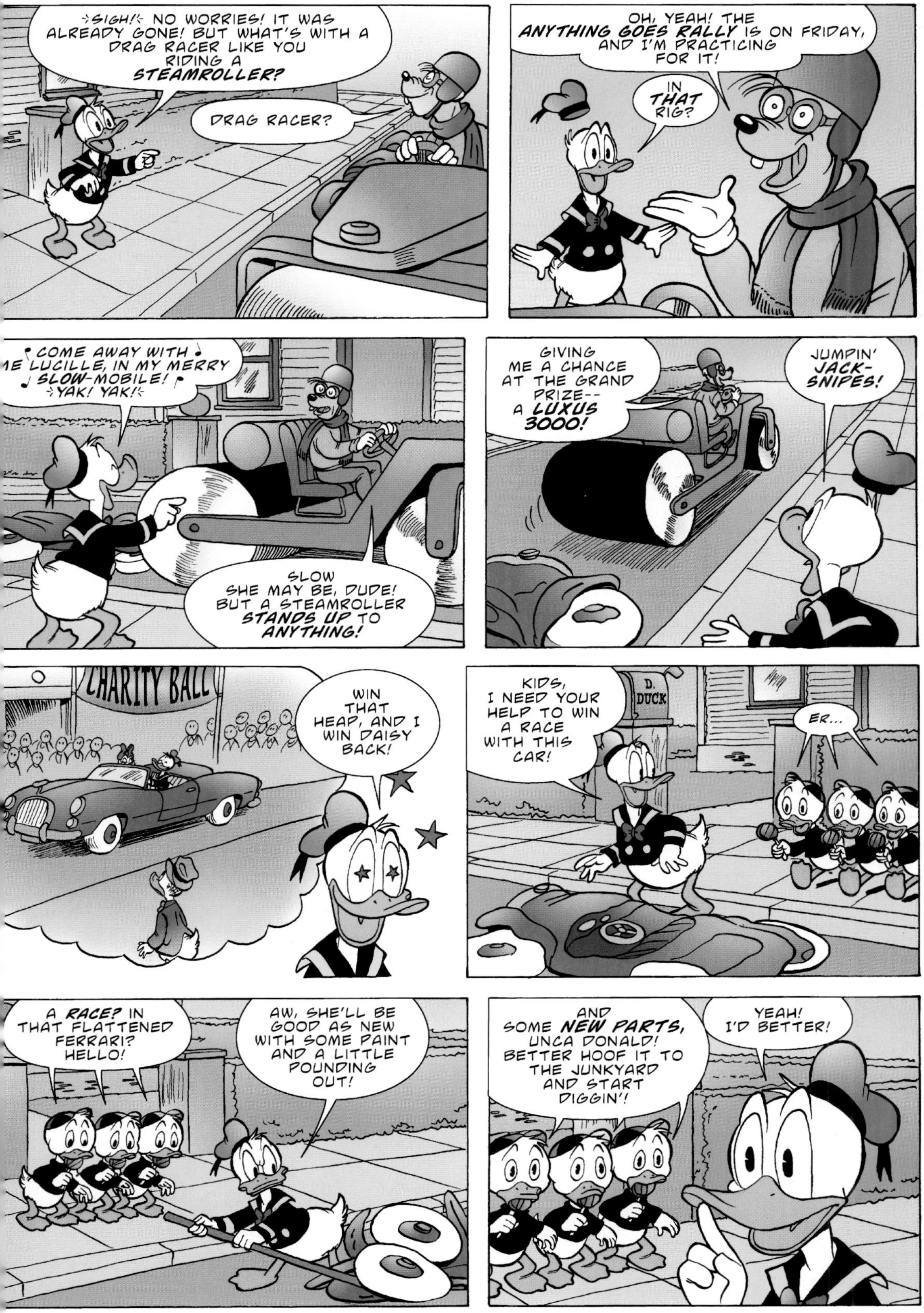

SIGH! NO WORRIES! IT WAS ALREADY GONE! BUT WHAT'S WITH A DRAG RACER LIKE YOU RIDING A **STEAMROLLER?**
DRAG RACER?
OH, YEAH! THE **ANYTHING GOES RALLY** IS ON FRIDAY, AND I'M PRACTICING FOR IT!
IN **THAT** RIG?
COME AWAY WITH ME LUCILLE, IN MY MERRY **SLOW**-MOBILE! *YAK! YAK!*
SLOW SHE MAY BE, DUDE! BUT A STEAMROLLER **STANDS UP** TO **ANYTHING!**
GIVING ME A CHANCE AT THE GRAND PRIZE-- A **LUXUS 3000!**
JUMPIN' **JACK-SNIPES!**
CHARITY BALL
WIN THAT HEAP, AND I WIN DAISY BACK!
KIDS, I NEED YOUR HELP TO WIN A RACE WITH THIS CAR!
D. DUCK
ER...
A **RACE?** IN THAT FLATTENED FERRARI? HELLO!
AW, SHE'LL BE GOOD AS NEW WITH SOME PAINT AND A LITTLE POUNDING OUT!
AND SOME **NEW PARTS,** UNCA DONALD! BETTER HOOF IT TO THE JUNKYARD AND START DIGGIN'!
YEAH! I'D BETTER!

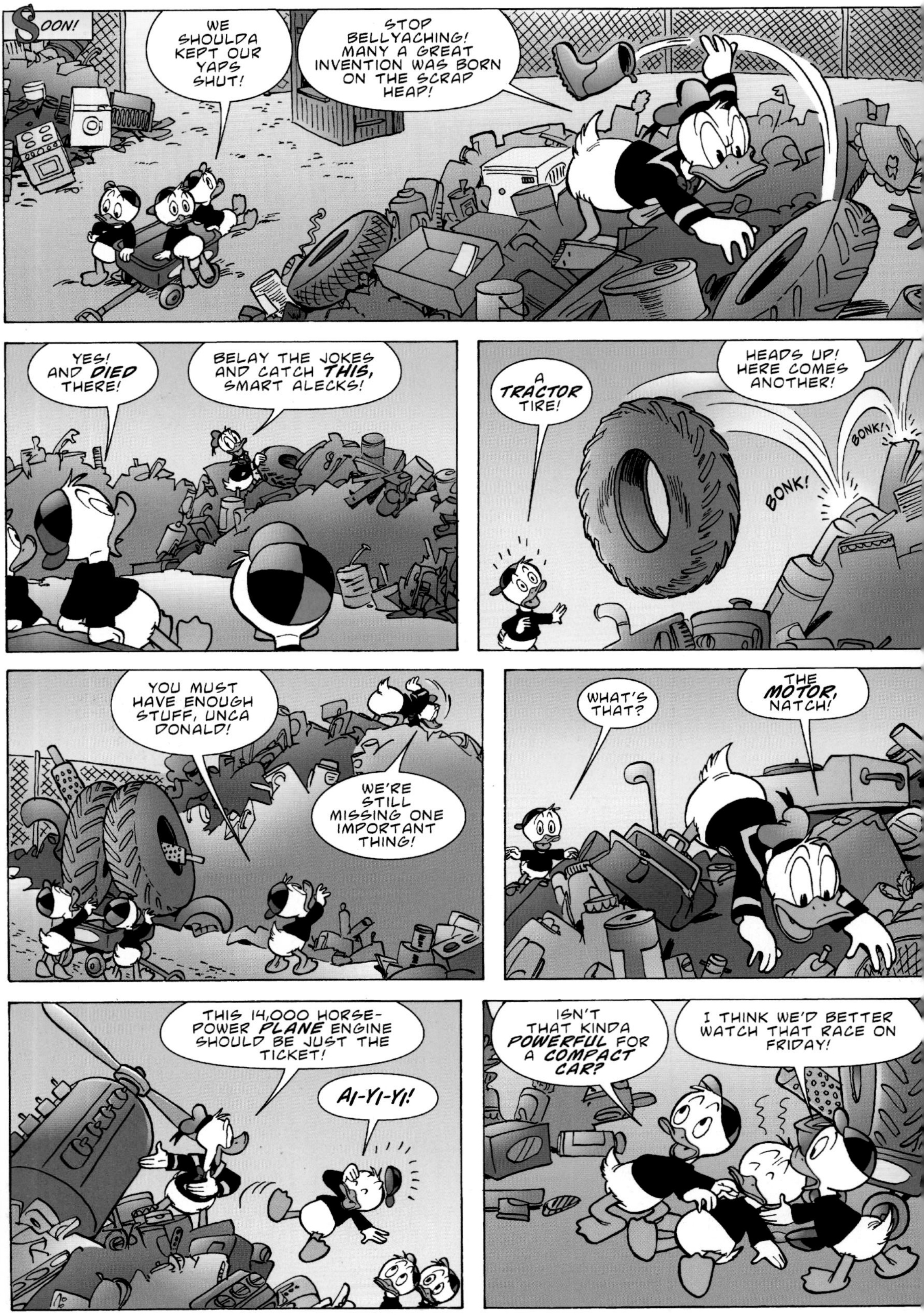
SOON!
WE SHOULDA KEPT OUR YAPS SHUT!
STOP BELLYACHING! MANY A GREAT INVENTION WAS BORN ON THE SCRAP HEAP!
YES! AND DIED THERE!
BELAY THE JOKES AND CATCH THIS, SMART ALECKS!
A TRACTOR TIRE!
HEADS UP! HERE COMES ANOTHER!
BONK!
BONK!
YOU MUST HAVE ENOUGH STUFF, UNCA DONALD!
WE'RE STILL MISSING ONE IMPORTANT THING!
WHAT'S THAT?
THE MOTOR, NATCH!
THIS 14,000 HORSE-POWER PLANE ENGINE SHOULD BE JUST THE TICKET!
AI-YI-YI!
ISN'T THAT KINDA POWERFUL FOR A COMPACT CAR?
I THINK WE'D BETTER WATCH THAT RACE ON FRIDAY!

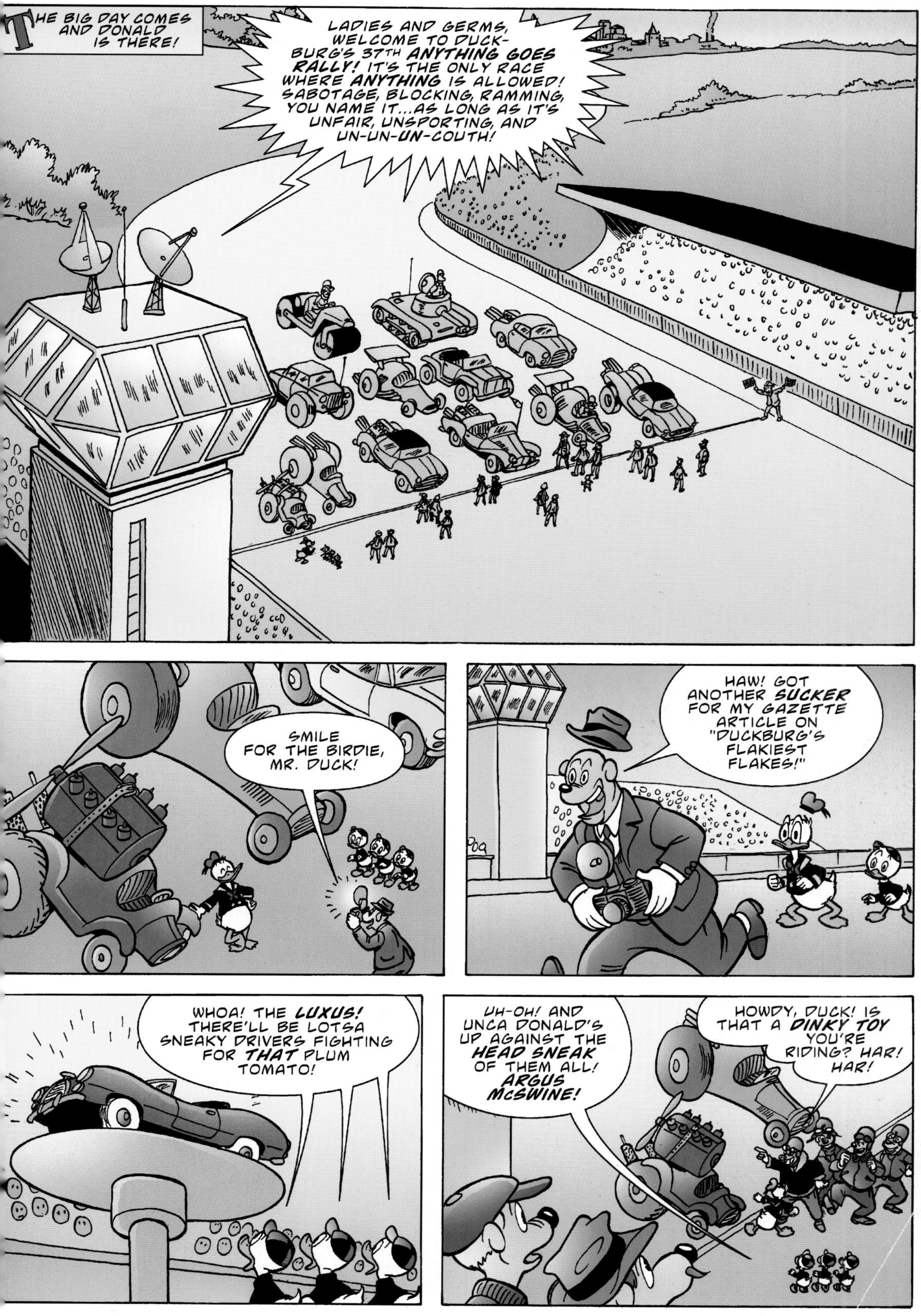
THE BIG DAY COMES AND DONALD IS THERE!
LADIES AND GERMS, WELCOME TO DUCKBURG'S 37TH ANYTHING GOES RALLY! IT'S THE ONLY RACE WHERE ANYTHING IS ALLOWED! SABOTAGE, BLOCKING, RAMMING, YOU NAME IT...AS LONG AS IT'S UNFAIR, UNSPORTING, AND UN-UN-UN-COUTH!
SMILE FOR THE BIRDIE, MR. DUCK!
HAW! GOT ANOTHER SUCKER FOR MY GAZETTE ARTICLE ON "DUCKBURG'S FLAKIEST FLAKES!"
WHOA! THE LUXUS! THERE'LL BE LOTSA SNEAKY DRIVERS FIGHTING FOR THAT PLUM TOMATO!
UH-OH! AND UNCA DONALD'S UP AGAINST THE HEAD SNEAK OF THEM ALL! ARGUS McSWINE!
HOWDY, DUCK! IS THAT A DINKY TOY YOU'RE RIDING? HAR! HAR!

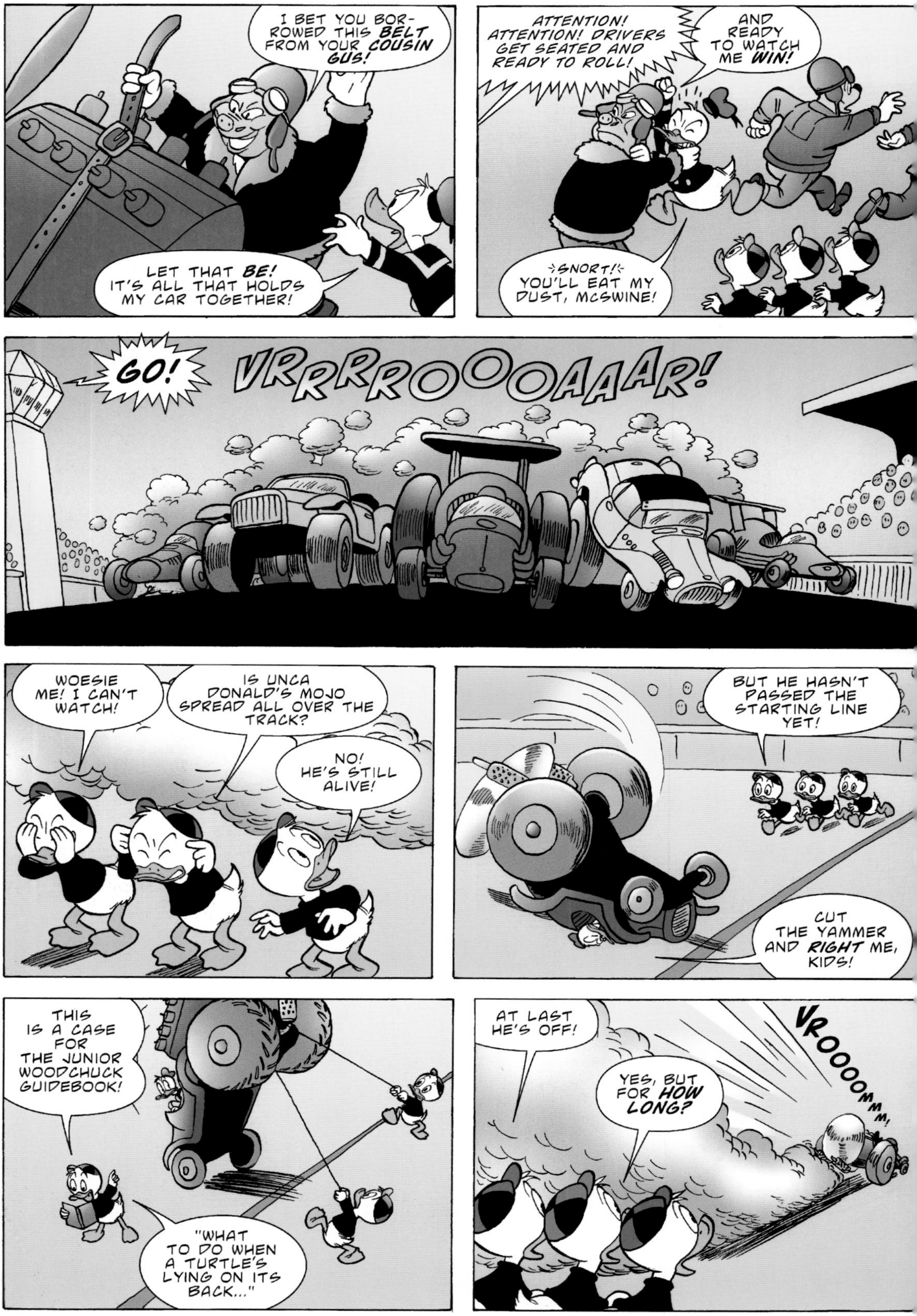
I BET YOU BORROWED THIS BELT FROM YOUR COUSIN GUS!
LET THAT BE! IT'S ALL THAT HOLDS MY CAR TOGETHER!
ATTENTION! ATTENTION! DRIVERS GET SEATED AND READY TO ROLL!
AND READY TO WATCH ME WIN!
SNORT! YOU'LL EAT MY DUST, McSWINE!
GO!
VRRRROOOOAAAR!
WOESIE ME! I CAN'T WATCH!
IS UNCA DONALD'S MOJO SPREAD ALL OVER THE TRACK?
NO! HE'S STILL ALIVE!
BUT HE HASN'T PASSED THE STARTING LINE YET!
CUT THE YAMMER AND RIGHT ME, KIDS!
THIS IS A CASE FOR THE JUNIOR WOODCHUCK GUIDEBOOK!
"WHAT TO DO WHEN A TURTLE'S LYING ON ITS BACK..."
AT LAST HE'S OFF!
YES, BUT FOR HOW LONG?
VROOOOOMMM!

I LOST HALF AN HOUR WITH THAT MEGA-LATE START! I'LL POUR ON THE GAS TO MAKE UP FOR IT!
THAT DUCK WANTS TO CUT IN BETWEEN US!
LET HIM TRY! WE'LL MASH HIM FLAT! HAW! HAW!
HOLY MOLEY!
ACK!
ONE SIDE, TURTLE BOYS! YOU'RE HOLDING UP THE RACE!
VUH-RROOOM!
WAS THAT THE DUCK?
IT LOOKED LIKE A COMET!
THAT WINDY DUCK IS CHASING MY TAIL! I'LL PUNCH A FEW HOLES IN HIS PRIDE YEK! YEK!
TACKS! TIME TO THINK FAST!
LOOK! HERE COMES THAT DUCK!
HEADED RIGHT FOR A BLOW-OUT!
OR NOT! EVEN TACKS CAN'T HURT THOSE TRACTOR TIRES!
AND HE WAS SMART...DRIVING ON JUST HIS BACK WHEELS!

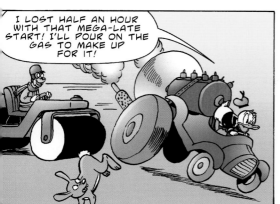

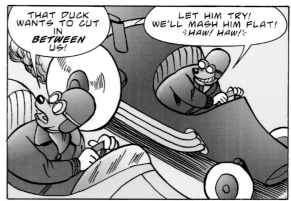

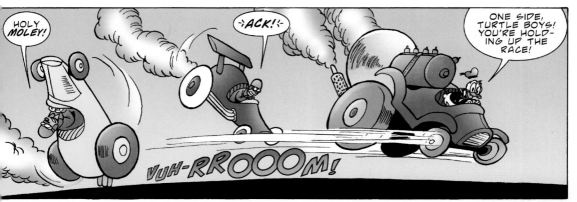

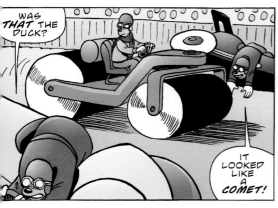

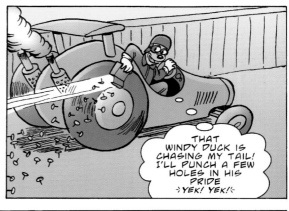

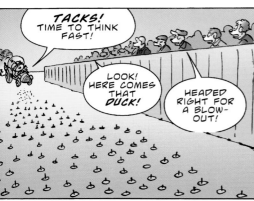

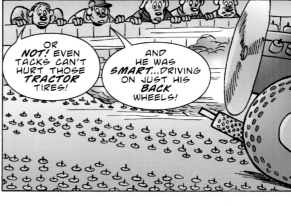

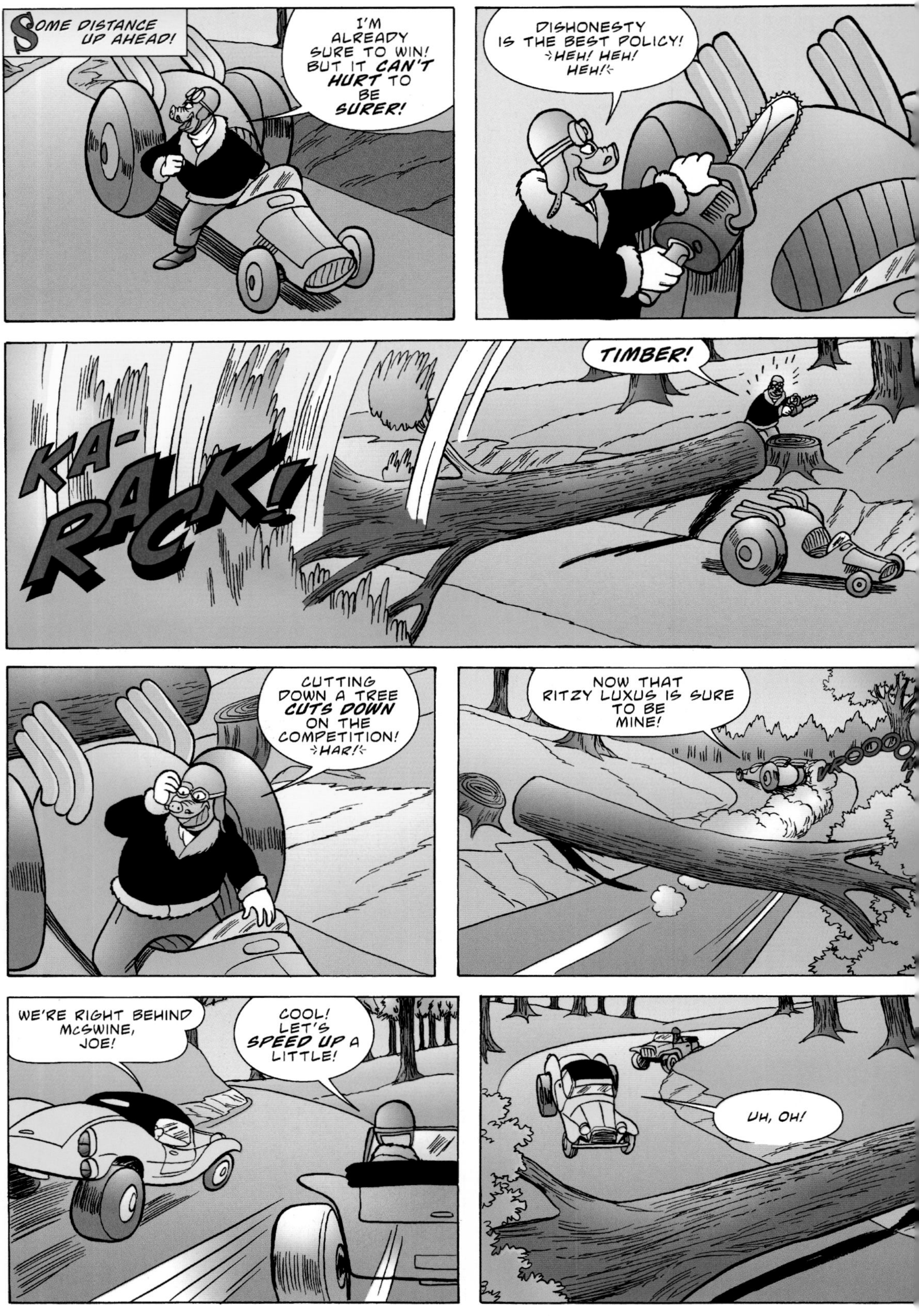

SOME DISTANCE UP AHEAD!
I'M ALREADY SURE TO WIN! BUT IT CAN'T HURT TO BE SURER!
DISHONESTY IS THE BEST POLICY! HEH! HEH! HEH!
TIMBER!
KA-RACK!
CUTTING DOWN A TREE CUTS DOWN ON THE COMPETITION! HAR!
NOW THAT RITZY LUXUS IS SURE TO BE MINE!
VROOOOM!
WE'RE RIGHT BEHIND McSWINE, JOE!
COOL! LET'S SPEED UP A LITTLE!
UH, OH!

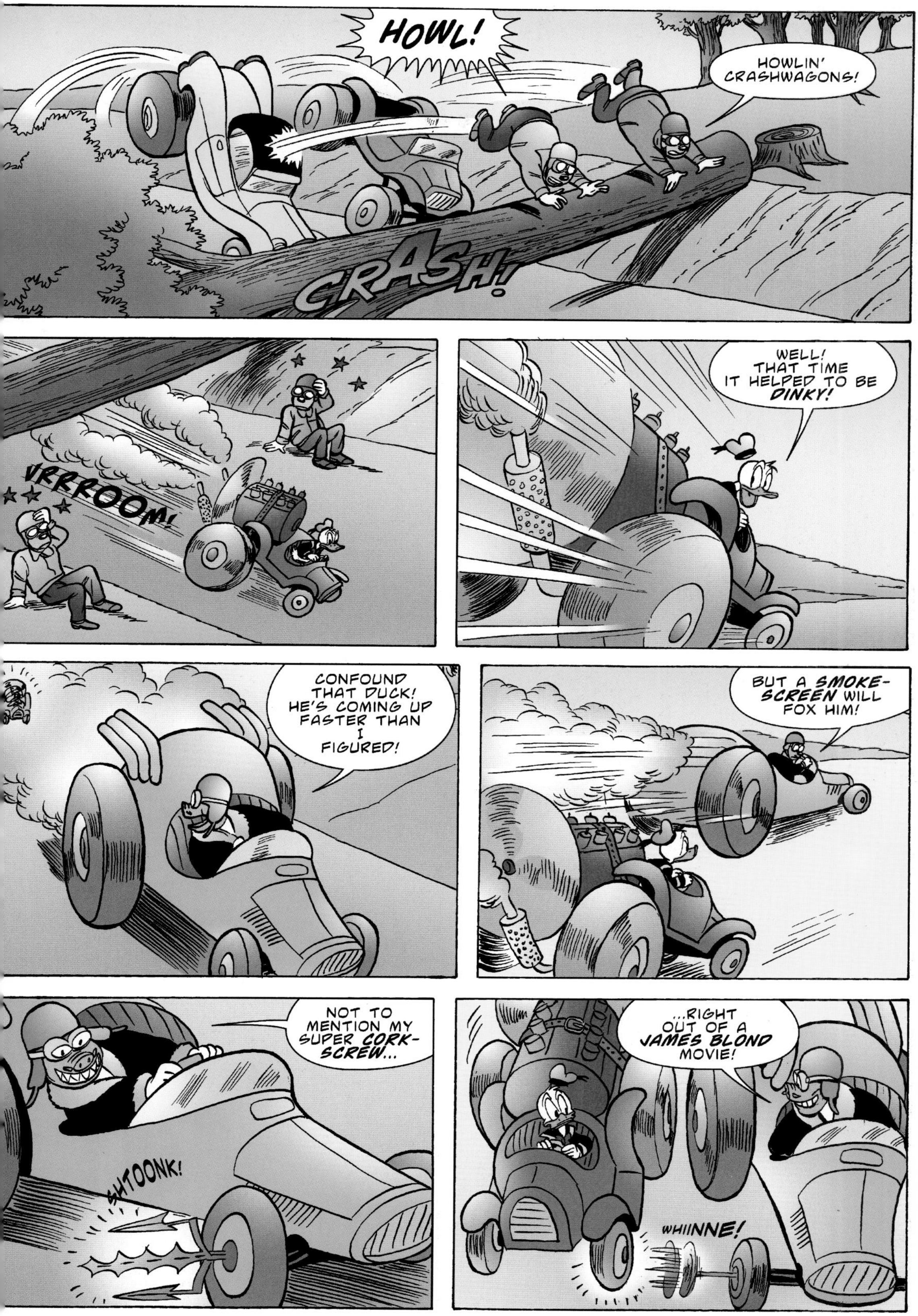
HOWL!
HOWLIN' CRASHWAGONS!
CRASH!
VRRROOM!
WELL! THAT TIME IT HELPED TO BE DINKY!
CONFOUND THAT DUCK! HE'S COMING UP FASTER THAN I FIGURED!
BUT A SMOKE-SCREEN WILL FOX HIM!
NOT TO MENTION MY SUPER CORK-SCREW...
SHTOONK!
...RIGHT OUT OF A JAMES BLOND MOVIE!
WHIINNE!

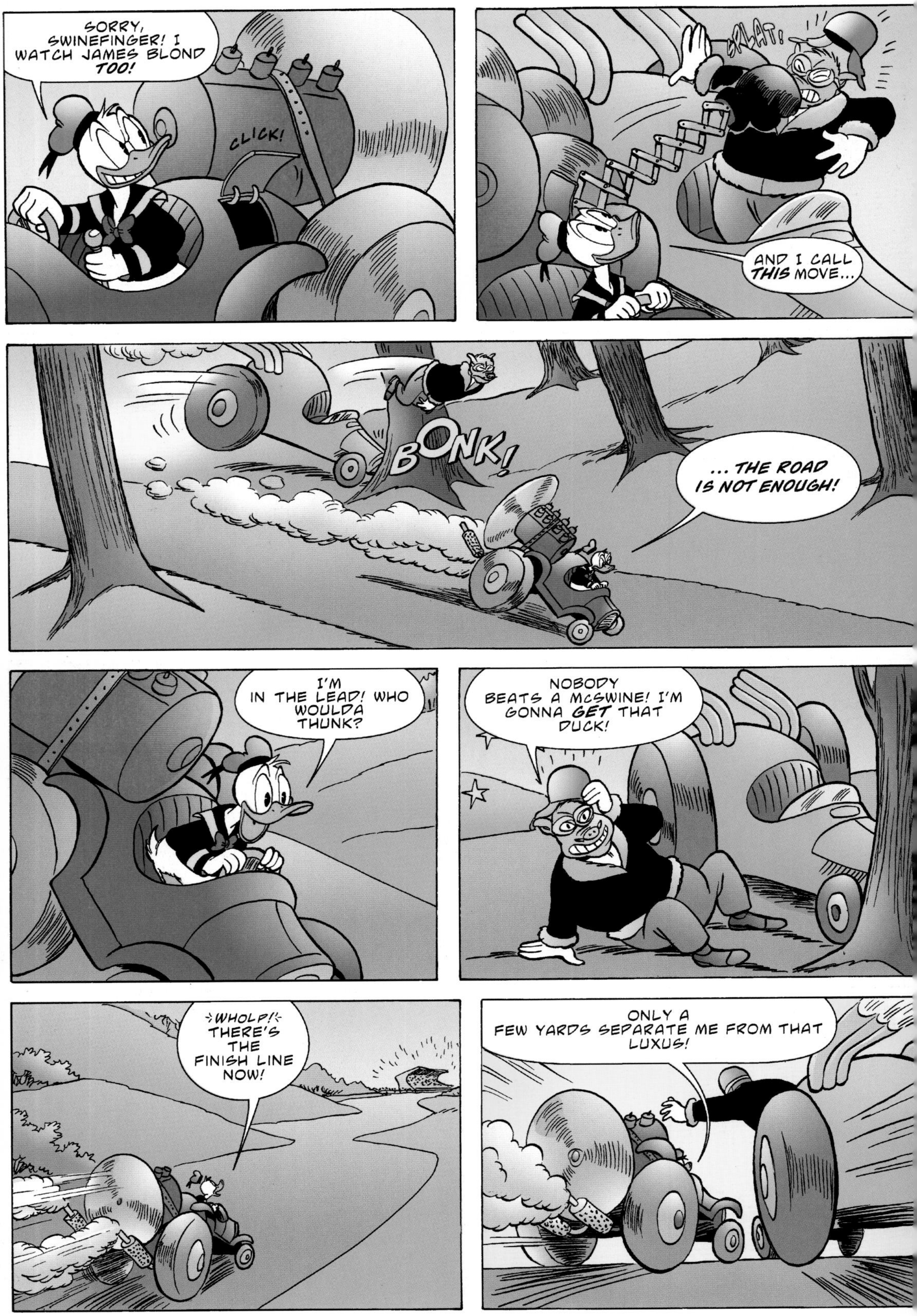

SORRY, SWINEFINGER! I WATCH JAMES BLOND TOO!
CLICK!
SPLAT!
AND I CALL THIS MOVE...
BONK!
... THE ROAD IS NOT ENOUGH!
I'M IN THE LEAD! WHO WOULDA THUNK?
NOBODY BEATS A McSWINE! I'M GONNA GET THAT DUCK!
WHOLP! THERE'S THE FINISH LINE NOW!
ONLY A FEW YARDS SEPARATE ME FROM THAT LUXUS!

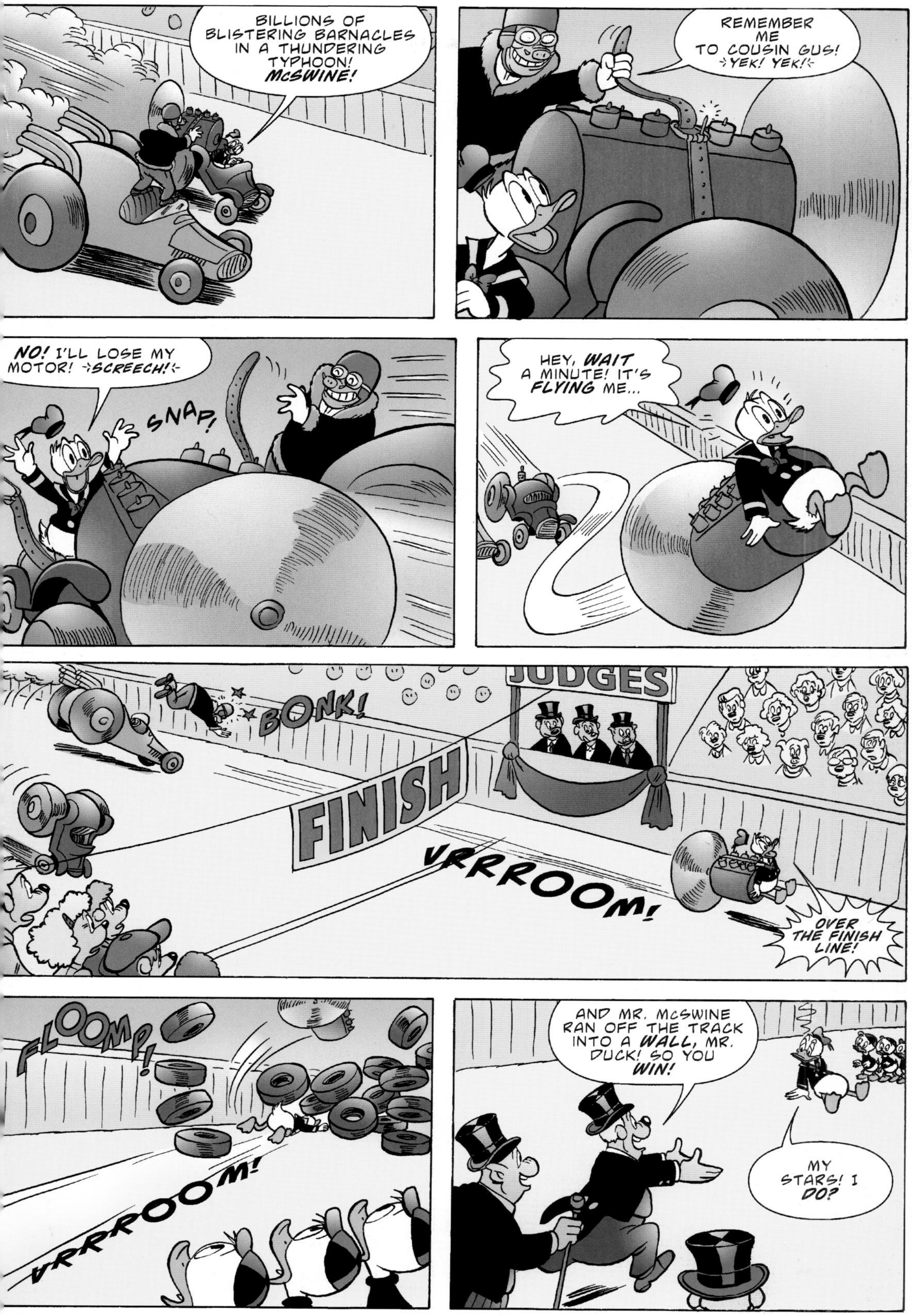
BILLIONS OF BLISTERING BARNACLES IN A THUNDERING TYPHOON! McSWINE!
REMEMBER ME TO COUSIN GUS! ~YEK! YEK!~
NO! I'LL LOSE MY MOTOR! ~SCREECH!~
SNAP!
HEY, WAIT A MINUTE! IT'S FLYING ME...
JUDGES
BONK!
FINISH
VRRROOM!
OVER THE FINISH LINE!
FLOOMP!
VRRROOM!
AND MR. McSWINE RAN OFF THE TRACK INTO A WALL, MR. DUCK! SO YOU WIN!
MY STARS! I DO?

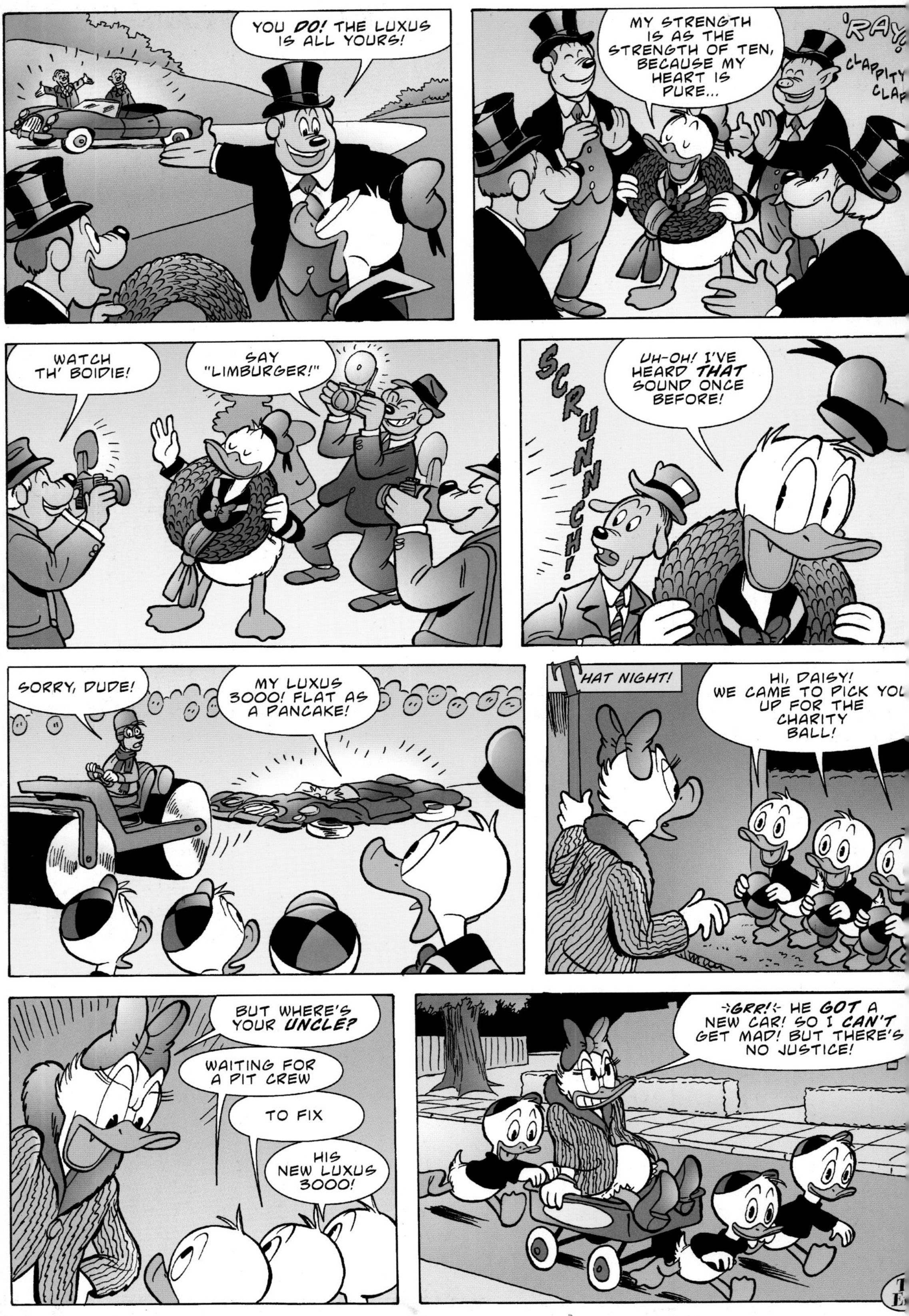

YOU *DO!* THE LUXUS IS ALL YOURS!
MY STRENGTH IS AS THE STRENGTH OF TEN, BECAUSE MY HEART IS PURE...
'RAY!
CLAPPITY CLAP
WATCH TH' BOIDIE!
SAY "LIMBURGER!"
SCRUNNCH!
UH-OH! I'VE HEARD *THAT* SOUND ONCE BEFORE!
SORRY, DUDE!
MY LUXUS 3000! FLAT AS A PANCAKE!
THAT NIGHT!
HI, DAISY! WE CAME TO PICK YOU UP FOR THE CHARITY BALL!
BUT WHERE'S YOUR *UNCLE?*
WAITING FOR A PIT CREW
TO FIX
HIS NEW LUXUS 3000!
GRR! HE *GOT* A NEW CAR! SO I *CAN'T* GET MAD! BUT THERE'S NO JUSTICE!